DELIGHTFUL
fear

A COLLECTION OF MACABRE TALES BY

AMANDA EAST

Copyright © 2019 Amanda East

ISBN: 9781701611405

DEDICATION

To three important men in my life:

To Stephen King for inspiring my dowsing rod moment,
To my husband for loving me even when I'm a little scary,
And to my dad for being the reason I love all things horror.

TABLE OF CONTENTS

WELCOME TO DELIGHTFUL FEAR

Anger in the face of threats.

A scream in the night.

The shiver of chilling intuition.

Uncontrollable shaking before a leap.

A lie of desperation.

Fear takes so many different shapes and sizes. How deeply we feel it and why it pounces on us entirely depends our own versions of terror.

Collected here in this little book are snapshots of fear from lives that are all so different, yet still consumed by the same basic emotion. It stands as a good reminder that no matter how different the things that drive and deter us, we all have one important thing in common...

We're all afraid of something.

Heartbroken

"And all I loved, I loved alone."
-Edgar Allan Poe

I have loved Lance Williams since I was 14 years old.

I fell for him in the middle school cafeteria during an 8th-grade dance where we shared our first kiss amidst the whispers and giggles of the whole student body. He never came to the school dances, but he came to this one for me, simply because he knew I was going to be there. We spent the night slow dancing and staring at each other with lovesick googly eyes like only children can. We said I love you after one kiss and thought we were so grown. We idealized young love but somehow made it last. That night started a love affair that I have invested my whole life into. That night changed my forever.

Through high school, we were a constant in each other's lives. We held hands down the hallways. He kissed me goodbye at all my classes. We were "that" couple for most of the four years and even in the brief moments we did split, everyone knew we would end up back together. We always did.

We were like fireworks. When we were together, we were making out in the backseat of his buddies car or rolling around in my bed during the few hours between school and my parents coming home. When we were broken up, we were screaming at each other in the parking lot or tearing each other's clothes off in the cab of his truck. We were on-again, off-again but always hot and heavy no matter what.

We just had this magnetic push and pull to one another. We couldn't stand to be apart, but sometimes we couldn't be together either. He had this intense power to make me feel like a queen or make me feel completely worthless depending on the day. Sometimes I think it was my own fault... I would get too clingy and he would tell me to back off. He would have a bad day and I would take it all too personally and cling again. I would say or do something stupid and he would tell me what a "miserable cunt" I was. Those were the times that it was so awful, but he always said he was sorry. He always came back and let me know he loved me. He always reminded me that I was his, for always.

Besides, that was just high school stuff. No relationship in high school is what it should be. We had so much time still to grow.

Eventually, we did grow out of all that back and forth nonsense and were together for good. My parents never liked him and didn't want me to see him, but Lance always reminded me that my family was there because they had to be. They were obligated because of DNA. He was the only one really there by choice and I would have to choose him if I wanted him to stay there. The harder they fought our relationship, the tighter Lance reeled me into his grasp. Eventually, he helped me make the choice to cut all ties with them. He was sure it was for the best and we moved in together right after we graduated. With my family, also went most of my friends as well. No one really understood our relationship, so it was just us after that.

Lance and I built a home together. We made a life, just the two of us. He loved me and I supported him so he could go to college. I didn't have a lot of work experience, but I was able to get a job at a little diner close to the university. Lance's parents weren't there much physically, but financially they helped us stay above water. Thanks to their generous allowance for Lance's college tuition, I was able to pay our bills by waiting tables so he could focus on his studies and start his career. When he was done with school, it would be my turn to go to college. He was going to make more money than me and we had his parents help, so it just made sense to let him go first.

He did graduate too, at the top of his class in business economics, but he thought it would be best if I stayed at the restaurant a while longer. He needed time to build the foundation of his career in financial planning and we didn't want to lose what little precious time we had with each other. He reminded me that if I went back to school while he was working so much, we would never see each other. So I stayed, cut my hours back, and took care of the house.

All my time and all my life have always been about him, but then he met Myra. Looking back, the day he met her I knew. I didn't know what I knew, but I knew something had shifted, something significant.

I noticed he started working even more than usual. He stopped coming home after work and would sneak into bed in the middle of the night. He would be gone again before I even woke in the morning. When he was home, he was cold and sometimes mean, or at least meaner than usual. I understood that he was under a lot of stress and that work was hard as he tried to get a new promotion, but I feared he was pulling away and fell into old patterns.

I clung to him at every moment. I texted incessantly. I called when he wasn't home. I met him at the door and slept only a few hours a night so that I could be there with him every moment possible. I morphed into this "desperate certified clinger" or at least that's what he called me.

Of course, he quickly grew more and more frustrated, pushing me away even more. He ignored my messages and let my calls go to voicemail. He would tell me to stop being such a "clingy loser". He told me how much of a nuisance I was in his life. He reminded me that he had left me before. What would stop him from doing it again? I felt like he wanted me to be there to care for our life, but he didn't want to be there with me.

I started walking on eggshells in my own home, terrified of breaking us further. I would rush home from work every day to fix my hair, do my makeup, and put on something sexy just to end up begging him to sleep with me. I would have done anything to bring him back. I just wanted to feel him close to me. The idea of losing him made me feel hopeless. He had always reminded me that no one else out there would ever want me like he did. Without him, I would be alone and I desperately wanted to avoid that solitude. I just wanted him to love me again, but the harder I tried, the farther I pushed him away.

As the months went on, I was consumed with so much self-hate and guilt. I felt like our current undoing was entirely on my shoulders. I felt like I had, in some way, failed him. I never imagined it was actually all because someone new was blowing him until I caught them in my own bed. His ass cheeks were clenched in ecstasy as he stood over the bed shoving his wad in her eager mouth.

I wasn't supposed to be there.

I was supposed to be at work for another two hours, plenty of time for them to finish their tryst without me ever knowing. If I had not been sent home after losing my lunch right there between two tables of mortified frat boys, I would never have known that it was even happening. I desperately wished I didn't. Ignorance is bliss, right, but it was too late for that.

Seeing the man I have given my whole existence to, giving himself so freely to another woman made the greasy queasiness climb back up my throat. I let out a squeak of disgust and threw my bags to the floor as I ran to the bathroom. I would assume I sent the lovers into a frenzy to try and hide their interlude, but from the moans and groans I heard, Lance wasn't phased a bit.

I spewed what was left of my lunch in the toilet probably at the precise moment he deposited a load of our unborn children down her throat. Not a single second was spared to consider my presence. He just didn't give a shit. I had literally walked in on him tearing our lives apart and he never once thought of me for even a second. I was completely shattered in that moment.

Myra was equally displeased and shouted obscenities at the man I loved. She called him a liar and a cheat. She told him he wasn't the man she thought she knew. She was crying hysterically as she slammed the apartment door that I paid for in his furious face.

That night we fought.

We screamed in each other's faces. I cried. He told me how it was all my fault entirely. How if I had been better he never would have had room in his heart for Myra. He told me it was too late. He had not only made room for her. He was in love with her. He told me she was better than I could ever even hope to be. He said he was leaving me.

That was it. That was the end. Everything I had built for us, everything I had sacrificed, everything I had created for him. It was all gone in the blink of an eye. He walked out the door and I fell to the floor. Sobs shook my body and self-hate tore through me, shredding my heart to pieces. I was beyond repair.

The pain was so intense that I found it hard to breathe. Something inside me knew that if I let go, the pain would take me. I would sink into its depths and never come back. It would eat me alive. I knew I had to find another emotion to cling to if I was going to survive. After everything I had invested into him I wasn't going to let this end me. Right then and there I latched onto a wave of fiery anger that was growing deep inside me.

As I let that dark heat fill me up, I began to reclaim a little bit of myself that I had forgotten ever existed. I remembered that I was the one that built this life for us. I remembered that I was the one that had made sacrifices. I had worked hard. I had made him what he was. He didn't define me. I defined him in every way. Fuck him if he thought I was going to let him flush all that down the toilet over someone he barely even knew. He owed me the rest of his life. His Myra hadn't done all the work I had to do to earn it.

That was my epiphany moment. A lightning rod to my core. Why had I let him do this to me? Why had I let him make me this weak, broken thing? I had given him too much and gotten nothing worthy in return. I had cheated myself on a deeper level than he could ever cheat me. I was officially letting him walk away with the spoils of the work I put into him.

Fuck that.

No.

Abso-fucking-lutely not.

I had a few drinks that night. I threw some things. I yelled and screamed at the top of my lungs, but then I made a plan. I was going to get him back one way or another. I had earned the right to his life and it was his turn to support me, whether he wanted to or not.

For the record, I want to be very clear, I was never angry with her. Myra was not where my furious thirst lied. She didn't do this to me and it would get me nowhere to waste time on hating her. I didn't know her. She didn't know me. She never intentionally meant to hurt me in any way. The only thing we shared in common was being duped and used by the man I had given my life to. Being his next intended crutch to support him through life was punishment enough for Myra.

Instead, my anger was placed directly and solely on Lance's shoulders. The situation he created was the catalyst for my crumbling life. I didn't want to walk away from him, I just wanted my turn and he owed me that. I wanted my life back and I wanted my turn to build something while letting him carry the weight of responsibility for once.

I hated him and what he had done to us, but I loved him too. It was a very complicated sea of emotions to understand what it meant to want someone so badly, even though the thought of them made you feel like tearing their throat out just to watch them slowly bleed out at your feet. Only this many years of loving someone could make you feel both homicidal and matrimonial all at the same time.

The next morning I woke with puffy eyes, a hangover, and a steely resolve in my gut. I was ready and prepared to fight with everything I had to have him back. He was mine, for better or for worse.

I'll be honest, I went a little nuts at that point.

I called him over and over again every single day. I left him lengthy voicemails when my calls were always immediately sent to voicemail. I cried. I yelled. I pleaded. I told him that he was mine and that he was never going to be rid of me because he owed me his life. I told him that he was going to realize someday how much he needed me in his life. I told him how much I hurt, how much my heart ached being away from him.

I texted him "I love you" and "I miss you" at all hours of the day and night. I typed out message after message detailing my rage, heartbreak, and total loss of understanding. I sent kisses. I sent old pictures. I sent hate-filled exclamations of betrayal.

I finally got a response when I sent him a picture of the positive pregnancy test I took on day 17 of the separation. Then we both knew why I had been throwing up around the clock. He called me immediately to berate me for trying to trap him. He was livid. He shot his sticky load inside me without the safety of a condom even though I had told him, again and again, I didn't want that and he was angry with me. He put a baby in my womb, but he was yelling at me.

I wanted to lose my shit right then, right there. Just throw my hands in the air and say fuck it all, fuck him, but I didn't. I had a plan by that point and I had no choice but to see it through. I was committed. That's clearly something I excel at.

So I took a deep breath and remained calm. I played up the heartbreak role and appealed to his self-love. I told him I had just been crazy over losing him and it was so hard because he was more than I could ever hope for in a partner. I told him I would do whatever he wanted and needed from me. I told him I would have an abortion and move on if he would just come to see me one last time so I could have closure. He was reluctant, but he agreed. I think a part of him kind of loved all the drama anyway. It made him feel good about his narcissistic self to know that I still wanted him. He got off a little on my pain and longing which just made the fury sizzle even hotter inside me.

Fuck that fucking douchewad, but he finally made good on his promise and came over earlier tonight. It's Valentine's Day today and I was amazed that he agreed to give up the ultimate date night for his expectant baby momma. As much as I hate to admit it, it gave me that warm fuzzy feeling to know he would still give me this day. Maybe he did still love me.

I made us a special dinner for two and had the whole scene set before he arrived. I wanted to give us a reminder of why we worked in the beginning. I didn't know how he would react, but I knew it would be a night to remember either way and he is sitting across the table from me right now so I'm happy with the result.

He was really reluctant at first. We fought, of course. He rolled his eyes at me and that was the moment that the last of my sanity cracked and splintered. My vision went red and I kind of blacked out for a minute, but now here we are.

His deep blue eyes stare unblinkingly into mine. I think he finally understands that I refuse to just be a passing memory in his life.

I peer up at him with a sultry stare as I feel the power I gained tonight fill my whole soul up. The candlelight glow makes the blood dripping from his mouth glimmer and I feel a spark of laughter uncontrollably spill out of me. I am certain I have truly gone mad, but he doesn't complain so I guess I'll just go ahead and lean into the crazy.

I cut another piece of tender flesh from my plate and savor the buttery salt taste melting over my tongue. I haven't enjoyed a meal this deeply in years. I rub a hand over my barely-there bump and delight in knowing that our little womb nugget is loving this meal with daddy too.

Having him here and having our rightful places in this relationship officially established sets everything in the world right. He looks defeated with shoulders slumped, still staring blankly across the table at me. Maybe I should feel bad for bringing him down, but it's really just that he finally understands now that I won't be taken for granted anymore. Never again. He needed to come to that realization.

His pale complexion and lifeless posture show his commitment to our new arrangement. No more fight in him. He's mine now in a deeper way than he's ever been before.

I let my eyes wander appreciatively down his body. I smile sinisterly to myself as my eyes reach his chest. The gaping hole of torn back flesh, bloody and still oozing his life force, gives me such intense joy. His heart used to rest there, beating only for me. Now his chest sits empty and I have absolutely no regrets over the alterations I have made.

I slide my knife through the tender meat on my plate once more before joyously indulging in another bite. As the flavor fills my mouth and washes over me I begin to laugh again, nearly hysterical.

I knew this night would be special. I knew it would be the night he gave his heart back to me. I just never imagined it would be on my plate.

I sit back serenely in my chair and embrace my teeny baby bump, lovingly stroking it.

Sweet, sweet baby. How does daddy taste?

Whiteout

"The future lies before you like a field of fallen snow."
-Unknown

The fog came first.

It descended on their sleepy town like a wool blanket, smothering out the ability to see more than a few feet at a time. It made itself at home and cozied in for the long haul without a moment of relief for 7 days. It only seemed to grow thicker as each day passed. Every surface was covered in dewy wetness. It was so intensely thick that you could almost reach out to grab it, but it was still just an inconvenience. Everyone still managed, just not quite as fast as their usual pace.

Their cars rounded the continual curves with more caution and concentration. They stayed a little closer to home and only ventured out in the moments of absolute necessity. Small adjustments were made to their lives, but they continued on. After all, it was just fog. Given time and the right forecast, it would be gone and they could go back to the regular hustle of modern living. They had absolutely no idea that the fog was only the opening act to the hell they were soon to discover.

When the moisture finally parted and the sun shone, warming their cold and damp souls, the temperatures soared to record highs. False hope felt so sweet on their skin that day. They all felt such intense relief to have normalcy back, but that one day was all it was. As the sun sank on the forested hills that evening the unseasonably warm temperatures plummeted to record lows. By morning, the sky was white again, this time with winter clouds blanketing the horizon. An arctic breeze seemed to be howling out a warning as it carried the clouds across the lake and towards the town.

It was like a monster lurking closer and closer every second. They all stood in awe as the suspension bridge tying their community to the rest of the world just disappeared in the white. Inch by inch the cold grey iron beams shrank away into nothingness. The scene was something out of a Stephen King novel and sank fear into every living soul watching.

The residents dropped everything they were doing and stared out at the white wall barreling toward them. The closer it came the louder it seemed to roar. Something internal, call it intuition, forced them all to feel a crawling chill working its way up their spines. They somehow knew this was more than just winter weather. It felt like it was coming for them.

As it slithered its way up the rocky cliff sides and forested hills, it seemed to put down roots, grinding to a halt directly above them. It was a complete whiteout of swirling, blizzard-like snow, the likes of which this little town had never seen before. Everyone sought out shelter anywhere they could and stood numbly watching waves of white flakes pelt their windows in a constant barrage.

Not everyone was lucky enough to immediately find their own desperately needed refuge. They were trapped too far out to make it to safety, but it was only snow. They would be fine, they were sure of it. Until they weren't.

Those on the lake were the first to feel the wrath. Their screams were heard briefly across the land, barely audible above the wailing whistle of the wind. A manic shriek against wintery skies was their last refrain. The wet splatter of their blood wasn't enough to be heard as the final warning to those still waiting.

Those sheltered away in warm homes now scrambled for their iPhones and Androids, wondering how they had missed the weather man's forecast calling for this unbelievable deluge of white, but all signal was lost and no internet connection could be found. They then turned on their TVs to tune into their local station for the inevitable winter weather warnings, but they seemed to have gone back in time displaying only white static fuzz matching the view outside. Radios were the next tech trend to be frantically tuned in only to find that nothing was decipherable but a loud whining tone drowning out all the voices. Those who still had home phone lines picked up their receivers to find that same whining tone reverberating in their ears.

The sound was otherworldly, causing the ears to bleed and the listener to lose all sense of comprehension. If they weren't able to pull themselves away from the tone it seemed to morph into something more sinisterly concrete. It came alive and coiled around their free will like a constricting serpent cutting off the ability to make rational decisions. Those poor souls stunned everyone around them when their expressions went slack and they walked directly out into the blowing snow. It was as if they had been possessed with a suicidal need that no amount of begging, crying, screaming, or coercion was going to disrupt. They simply walked straight out the door and become a part of the abyss, disappearing into the white, howling sheets of snow.

Seeing someone vanish into the blizzard shook onlookers to their core. In their hearts, they wanted to chase them down and drag them back from the cold kicking and screaming, but something deep down and more powerful than the needs of the heart told them to stay rooted to the spot. It was a primal fear within them, the basic survival instinct, that made them know somehow that it was not safe in ways beyond rational reality, that if they walked out into that snow they would never come back. It was almost like they could feel the gaze of something out there watching them like a feral cat watches its prey, hunkered down in wait for the right moment to pounce.

Their intuition was right. This wasn't just snow or a crazy fluke of the weather. This storm had a real and tangible hunger. It wanted human flesh and had every intention of eating them all alive one way or another.

Staying inside during a snowstorm is never easy to do, but it can be done, at least for a little while. Eventually, we all have things to do, places to go, and jobs to report to. To lock yourself in for days with no outside contact can be excruciating and not possible indefinitely. As much as they feel like they shouldn't or as much as they don't want to, eventually everyone has to leave or risk starving inside.

The snow wasn't really piling up anywhere. It just seemed to be swirling around like they were trapped inside a rolling snowglobe. Everything seemed to be accessible, just white. When hunger and desperation really set in they, one by one, decided surely there could be no harm in facing the cold blowing wall of flakes... Five days in, those still remaining began disobeying their gut feeling and venturing out to gather food and supplies, to check on loved ones, or to attempt going into work.

Within just moments of leaving their safe places of warmth, they were snatched up and eaten alive. All that was left behind was snow stained blood red. A few of them saw their killers, but only when it was entirely too late to make any difference. Instead of escaping or winning a fight for their life, their last moments were filled with the soulless eyes of the ones that brought the snow.

All white and wispy, almost invisible except for their black, soulless eyes and gleaming silver fangs. Their teeth like daggers of dripping, molten steel tore out throats and made meals out of the innocent. They looked like nothing more than clouds possessed with evil incarnate. They were thin as air but held more power than any being on Earth ever had before. It was clear they were not of this world, but they would own in just a short while.

Once they had every last soul in the tiny town, the snow faded away into nothing, like it had never even been there. The sky cleared. The sun shined down on the empty streets. Life appeared to be returning to the cold and barren homes, but they all stood empty. As the snow melted away into the ground, so too did the red splashes of spilled life, erasing all evidence of the massacre that residents suffered.

Life carried on all around the death ridden town. The world kept spinning. No one even knew what had happened there. It was as if the whole world forget it had ever existed. It was now just another forgotten town in a rural graveyard.

People passed through and wondered what would make a whole town disappear. Sometimes they told their own stories and made up plausible explanations of their very own, but they never even came close to the truth. They never knew what really happened.

At least not until it was their town's turn because this rural massacre was only the prelude, a mere testing of the waters. One by one, this wall of white crawled its way through the human race and left no survivors. Our planet became just the next forgotten world, cold and barren like all the ones before it.

The Wicked Seed

"Destroy the seed of evil, or it will grow up to your ruin."
-Aesop

Have you ever had something specific come across one of your five senses and it completely transports you to a different time and place?

In early August of every year, I travel back to my fourth year as a kindergarten teacher. I remember the thick heat of summer boiling onto its hottest days in a classroom where air conditioning wasn't a priority just yet. I can smell the dust from fresh chalk in the air mixing with the stench of summer break's disinfectant still rising from the desks. I hear the giggles and uncertainty of the promise in a new year of growth and learning. It was one of my favorite times of the year and something I genuinely looked forward to all summer. A new school year, a whole classroom full of new eager faces, and brand new memories to be made, but that one year in particular year was different.

It sent me down a path that changed who I was inside, even though I never really grasped what it all meant back then. Not until today, 16 years later. I don't think I wanted to know. I think I wanted to leave my head buried in the sand; the warm, safe, and delusional sand. He didn't let me do that though and now I am whirling in the memory of how frightened I had been of him when he was just 5 years old.

His name was Alexander, but he went by Lex or so his mother told me on his first day in Kindergarten. He had not been enrolled before the first day of school and wasn't on my roster so I hadn't expected him. An hour into that very first day for a new class of children, his mom had personally walked him to my room tightly grasping his hand and looking more nervous than he was. She fretted constantly through the drop-off and admitted that she had been unsure of bringing her "special boy" at all. It was clear immediately that he was the one in charge of that relationship. Having worked with children this age my entire adult life, I had a radar for different behaviors. This guy was spoiled rotten.

I initially thought he was likely an only child, but his mom let me know that he had recently become a big brother for the first time. That seemed to be rubbing him the wrong way judging from the sour expression and eye roll he gave in response to his little sister's sweet name, Luna. Lex was not a fan of Luna just yet. I giggled at this because it was a hard thing for kids this age who had always been the apple of their parent's eyes to suddenly be thrust into "neglected" older sibling mode.

I assured mom with a sweet smile that he would be

perfectly fine in my care and that I looked forward to getting to know him. Which, at the time, was completely true. I had never really encountered a student that I couldn't love or embrace for their varied little personalities. There would always be some students that were more challenging than others, but I cared about them just the same. I loved it all when it came to being a teacher and my students were what made it so much fun. Of course, they all had their moments where you felt like you may be crazy before they went home for the day, but all in all, I would never have wanted to be doing anything else with my life.

I immediately thought that Lex was going to join my growing list of lovable troublemakers. He had a constant sparkle of what I thought was mischief in his eyes, yet he was unbelievably charming. I think the charm had a lot to do with how incredibly beautiful he was in a really powerful way. He was simply gorgeous, especially for a child of his age. Golden blonde hair, rosy cherubic cheeks, the biggest blue eyes you've ever seen framed by mile long, dark black eyelashes. He was an angel or so he appeared.

He kept me fooled for the first couple of months. He was just so dang sweet and I just wanted to love on him all the time. He always said the right things and seemed to be such a charismatic little guy. You couldn't help but love him. He was so kind and attentive to the girls in our class. I really felt like he was going to make a wonderful husband and father someday.

What a freaking joke.

It was around early November when I got the first glimpse of the real person inside the mask he wore every day. My class was in their specials which meant I was without them for one whole hour. I had not quite made it back from the copy room when they started their walk back to our room with the music teacher. Lex was bringing up the end of the line with his sweet little friend Mya and as the class stopped at the end of the hall to wait for me these two happened to be right outside the copy room door with no clue that I was hidden away inside. I smiled at first to see the darling pair approaching hand in hand, but what I heard next completely stunned me because what I was witnessing was so out of character for who I thought he was.

"You are just stupid, Mya. No one else wants to be your friend because you are just plain dumb. That's why you have to stay close to me. I know how stupid you are too, but I still put up with you," he trilled in his sweet five-year-old pitch. "You don't need other friends anyway. I am all you need. I'm the only one that wants to be friends with a dumb bitch like you."

My hand flew to my mouth and I just stood there unable to move as I listened to the words so casually fall from his mouth. It wasn't that the sentiment of "you're stupid" or the use of a swear word was so out of the realm for a kindergartner to say. It wasn't at all, to be honest. I heard it a million times in one variation or another over the course of a school year. It was simply the accurate use and manipulative way in which he was expressing it. He felt safe from prying adult ears and took full advantage of the moment. It was hurtful and effective in ways a child this young should never understand. Sweet Mya looked so dejected and sad. One look in her little face and I was out the door.

"Alexander Wilson! I better not hear you speaking to a friend in that way ever again," I screeched as they both turned to face me with frightened faces thanks to my abrupt outburst. "Do you understand me?"

He looked sheepish for only a moment and a little redness crawled into his cheeks. I thought, at the time, that it was embarrassment from being caught in such a nasty moment. Now I realize that it was more likely anger at me for calling him out so publicly.

"I-I... uh..." he stammered, looking for the right response. "I didn't mean it. I was joking!"

His bubbly giggles burst out with his words and a genuine smile. It softened me for a moment, just a small moment. That was the moment that I turned on my radar for Alexander Wilson. He had so charmed me and everyone else in his life, that a sweet smile and a simple laugh was enough to make me want to forgive him for the awful things he had just said. I knew at that moment that maybe something about him was different. I don't know how I knew it, but I just had that gut feeling.

I didn't let him off the hook. I followed through on a long talk about inappropriate interactions with peers and time out, as well as a note home to mom and dad. Sitting in that time out chair for the first time ever in his little schoolboy career, I believe Lex changed the way he looked at me as well. As he stared me down from across the room, it appeared he had decided I was no longer an ally to him. He was looking at me with a new fire in his eyes. I was the enemy now.

From then on Lex and I seemed to be playing a game of who would blink first. I would catch him in a frighteningly menacing situation and we would lock eyes. We both knew what was going on and neither wanted to let the other side win. Over time, as I witnessed more and more of his inner self, I became a little frightened of him. He was just so good at what he did.

I spoke to his parents about his behavior and asked if they had witnessed anything similar at home. They stared at me completely offended that I would even suggest their golden boy was anything other than absolutely perfect. They had never seen him, or so they said, behave in a less than exemplary manner at any point in his entire life. I had to work really hard to contain my eye roll on that one...

I decided to reach out to other teachers and our administrators at that point, but got all the same brush offs:

"But he's such a sweetheart!"

"Don't worry so much! I'm sure it's nothing."

"He's too cute to be that mean!"

"You must watch too many Dateline Mysteries!"

After a while, my peers began to question my fitness as a teacher. Our administrators wondered if I needed a break from the profession. Serious whispers in the halls began about whether or not I was cut out for teaching. If I could let one child who may or may not have a "couple quirks" define my ability to successfully teach, then could they all trust me as a member of their school team?

I grew very frustrated very quickly. I became afraid to speak to anyone about it anymore and kind of isolated myself from those I worked with, out of fear of ridicule. I even started to question myself on a couple of occasions, but every time I did he would completely reaffirm all my suspicions.

I was becoming more and more certain by the day that this child in my classroom was a budding psychopath with the potential to be a very dangerous person without the right kind of intervention. The problem was, I couldn't get him the intervention he needed if no one took his behaviors and my pleas seriously, which they clearly didn't.

He was just so darn good at playing the role of darling child. He could turn on the charm at the drop of a hat and leave everyone sure he was a rare gift to this earth. He would still have me fooled too if I hadn't caught him. That was the only reason he didn't work to hide his behaviors from me anymore. He knew he had nothing to hide from me. I already knew and he seemed to change his tactic from charming me into loving him as he did with others, to trying to frighten me into submission. He chose moments that he knew I was watching to display some of his worst indiscretions. He wanted to shock me and, honestly, it worked most of the time.

It was more than just the things he said and did as well. It was the way he looked at me when he was in the middle of his behaviors. It was like he could see right through me. He wasn't looking at me, he was looking inside me to see exactly what it was he could take from me to ruin me. It sounds absurd to say a kindergartner had the ability to do that, but if you could have seen it you would have said the same. I promise you, he was different. He was not like the other kids. He had something inside him that was pure evil in the most basic of ways.

Ha... Even hearing myself tell you all this, I know I sound crazy. I absolutely know it sounds insane. If I were you I would feel the same way, but I swear to you, if you had been there you would understand.

One morning, in particular, I remember he came into the classroom with a huge smile on his face, handing me a note from his mother. She had written to let me know that his beloved cat, Simon, had died and poor, heartbroken Lex had been the one to find him. He had, apparently, been inconsolable and she was worried that he may have a hard time throughout the school day. She had been prepared to keep him home for the day, but he had begged to come. She relented believing it may provide a good distraction for him. As I read the words his mother had written I felt Lex watching me. I peered up at him and shivered at the cool and collected smile on his angelic face.

"Do you want me to tell you the sound he made when he hit the sidewalk outside my bedroom window?" Lex asked me with a gleam in his bright blue eyes. "Or how much he fighted me when I was throwing him out the window?" My blood went cold and I sucked in a harsh breath. It thrilled him to see me like this. His smile darkened further and he spoke in a low tone, "Do you want to know what dead smells like?"

"Alexander, stop," I blurted too loudly, causing the other children in the room to turn and stare, but he wasn't phased. He loved it.

"You can tell on me, but nobody will believe you," he spoke sweetly and I knew he was right. I had tried and no one had believed me yet. What would change that now? Most thought I was crazy or had some ridiculous agenda against a five-year-old boy.

That was a different time. It wasn't like now when all the classrooms and hallways are monitored with high tech camera systems. We didn't all carry around smartphones back then. If he had come into my life in the last handful of years I would have had him recorded in his terrifying moments before he could blink, but back then all I had was my word against his and you would be amazed how many adults will side with a child over a trained professional.

That morning he ran off to play with the other precious children in my room and I wished there was some way I could save them or shelter them all from this evil boy. I had no doubt that just being in his presence regularly was going to damage them, but what could I do? He had them all manipulated too and they would never turn on him. He was a user and an abuser. That's what they do. The best I could do was just stand vigil and try to prevent any further mind play.

It didn't matter if it was major or minor, I was all over him.

I caught him giving Evie his best puppy dog eyes at lunch so she would give him the fruit roll-up from her lunch box and swooped in with a reprimand. I heard him telling

Charlie that he wouldn't be friends with him anymore if he didn't give Lex the kickball at recess and I blew the whistle to disperse the crowd. I snatched him up and plopped him in time out when he "accidentally" tried to cut Cynthia's ponytail off during arts and crafts. I quarantined him from his classmates for the rest of the afternoon when I overheard him quizzing Thomas, "What would happen if you cut your dog's tongue out?". I even made the rest of the day mandatory rest time for the whole class just to process what had happened the day I caught him using Barbies to show Jamie how he would peel away her skin just like his father skinned a deer.

I was on constant high alert and never let my guard down for even a second, but in a busy kindergarten classroom, you can so easily be distracted. I hope that I did my best to protect the rest. I'm sure I will ponder that for the rest of my life.

It was enough stress that school year that I started losing my hair. Nearly all of my eyebrows fell out. I had chewed all my nails down to bloody stubs. My husband stood behind me and helped with our 3-year-old at home, but outside of that safety net I was a mess because I had no allies among my coworkers. They had all written me off as the crazy one.

Lex was not in the best of mental states either. His resentment for me was growing by the day. He was beyond tired of my micromanagement of his behaviors. Every time I stopped him in his deviant moments, he would glare at me. If looks could kill I would have been six feet under a long time ago. He let me know that many times.

"I don't like you," he stated point-blank to my face one afternoon while sitting in the time out chair I had relocated to directly by my desk. "You are messing up all my stuff and I don't want to be in your class no more."

I replied, "That's not a choice, Lex. We're just going to have to make the best of the rest of our time together."

He rolled his eyes and mumbled under his breath. I couldn't hear what he said and asked him to repeat himself. With a dark glare he spoke coldly, "I might not give you much more time."

I wanted it to not be a big deal. I wanted it to roll off me in its absurdity, but it chilled me to the core. If you had just known him… That was the day I knew he was out to get me in the literal sense. He wanted to rid his life of me and for the very first time in my life, I felt afraid of a five-year-old little boy. Outwardly, I brushed it off like it was all silly, but way back in the depth of my mind I was terrified, as ridiculous as that may sound.

The coming days did nothing to reassure me. I came into my room to find my chair broken and caught myself just before I fell into the scissors lodged blades up directly below it. I sliced my fingertips on a razor blade jammed into the handle of my desk drawer. I climbed the small ladder I used to reach the top shelf of my bookcase to find bolts had been removed causing me to tumble to the ground, narrowly missing a mirror that had been moved out of the dress-up corner. I was dumbfounded. I couldn't figure out how or when he was doing these things, but I had zero doubt that he was the one doing them.

Things were growing so terrible that I would sit in my car and cry at the end of each school day. I contemplated quitting but knew that leaving in the middle of a school year would be career suicide. I also knew it would mean he won and, looking at my sweet daughter's face, I couldn't bare letting someone like Lex beat me. If I gave up, who would stop him? So, instead of giving up I decided to become even more overbearing so he would never have a chance to create these moments of horror at all, at least not in my presence.

After a few days of my overachieving supervision, I really thought he would fall apart and show the world who he really was. He was growing that frustrated with me, but it turns out he knew how to change his tact as well. He came in the next morning and sweetly smiled at me. He walked over to my table and laid his baby blues on me with a dramatic batting of his eyelashes. I was suspicious immediately.

"I was wondering," he began in his best voice of innocence, "what it's like in your neighborhood." He peered up at me with the look of complete interest and wonder.

Nervously I responded, "What do you mean? What is what like in my neighborhood?"

"Like... what is there to do where your house is?"

Still unsure and not understanding where his questions were leading, I hesitated. He was still my student though and, at the end of the day, I would still treat him like any other beautiful and inquiring mind in my class. He deserved that from me no matter what I personally felt towards him. That was my job as an educator, so I answered, "Um... well, I live near a really nice park. I like to walk there sometimes."

"Is it a park here in this town with our school or another town?"

"It's... in another town," I responded and noticed that he looked let down by this answer.

He took a moment to think and then continued what was beginning to feel like an interrogation, "Is it a close city or a faraway city? Could you ride a bike there?"

I pondered this for a moment and started to answer, but decided to take a different route first, "Lex, why are you asking?"

He chewed his lip and paused for only a split second, but it was long enough for me to notice his hesitation, "I just thought it would be nice to talk about where we live, " he spoke, smiling serenely.

Uncertainty fueled me to answer his questions with questions of my own, "Well, why don't you tell me about where you live?"

A scowl preceded his response, "I would really just rather hear about your house. Where is it?"

"Lex, I don't really talk to my students about where I live. I like to keep a little mystery," I said with a smile and a wink to try and make him giggle like the other kids would.

He wanted nothing to do with my humor. He realized then that I wasn't going to give him any more information and he was livid. He shot out of his chair, slammed it against my table, and stomped across the room. He rooted himself into a chair in the reading center, arms folded across his chest. If looks could kill.

I sat still for several minutes letting the details of our conversation sink in. I truly think he was trying to find out where my house was and if it would be easy for him to get to. He was trying to find out where I live. I let out a deep sigh and shook off the interaction. I didn't want him to see that he had rattled me. That would give him satisfaction that I wasn't willing to award him with any more. I tried to just carry on with my day and did, for the most part, until our afternoon visit from the fire department.

Every year they came in and talked to the students about fire safety. The kids always loved to see the firefighters in their official equipment. These men and women were real-life superheroes and the kids became absolutely starstruck when they saw them. It was one of the highlights of the school year to see their little faces light up so brightly.

Even Lex was excited to see them and I was proud to see him sitting among his classmates watching in awe. It was such a sweet moment in a day that had started so differently. In that moment he was just another one of the kids and I didn't feel the need to shelter anyone from his influence.

The event went over as well as always. The firefighters were beginning to take questions from the kids and Lex shot his hand in the air, "Mister, how does a house catch on fire?"

I felt a chill roll down my spine. It was an innocent enough question from what appeared to be a normal kindergartener, but it triggered something in me. The firefighters took him completely serious and answered his question with great detail. When he saw this window of information flying open, I saw the sparkle in his eyes.

He smiled wickedly at me over his shoulder and began a barrage of questions he was undoubtedly storing for later use:

"What kind of stuff is flam... flan... flambleable?"

"How long until the fire trucks get there?"

"Can people really die in fires?"

"What happens if you can't get out of the house in a fire?"

As each one rolled off his tongue with a thirsty curiosity, I grew sick to my stomach. The firefighters told me I might have a future firefighter in my class. I gave a weak smile in response but couldn't bring myself to do much more. If they only knew.

Over the following days and weeks, Lex seemed to be in a great mood constantly. It made me nervous. He didn't try to pry the location of my home out of me anymore, but that didn't stop me from checking around corners and searching the whole house at the faintest hint of smoke. I was paranoid that he was coming for me and then, just like that, the world fell apart.

Have you ever started a day and just known that something significant would make it particularly memorable?

You just know this day will matter in some way. You have an undeniable gut feeling. On that bright April morning, I woke up with a weight on my chest and I just knew.

I took my time getting ready that morning. I was in no hurry to get to school which was unusual for me, but I just didn't want to be there that day. I was dreading it intensely and I didn't even know why. When I did finally get there I immediately wanted to turn around and go back home. The face of everyone in the administration office confirmed my fears. Heads were lowered. Tears streaked faces. Hugs were passed from one to another. Something awful had happened and it would affect all of us.

I walked wearily to my classroom and sank into my chair with my head in my hands, rubbing my temples. I was just bracing for the impact when our principal walked in and shut the door behind her. I felt instantly claustrophobic.

"Have you heard?" Her face was grave.

My heart sank, "I don't guess I have."

She heaved a sigh and continued, "There's been an... incident involving one of your students."

Don't say his name. Please do not say his name.

She tried to continue but had to take a moment to collect herself. Drawing in a deep breath, she wiped away the tears streaking down her cheeks nearly uncontrollably. Finally, she dropped the bomb, "Alexander Monroe's family has been in a house fire."

I gasped, but for entirely different reasons than she believed. She put her hand on my shoulder in a comforting gesture. I was tense and bracing for the rest of the story because I knew without a single doubt, there would be more.

"His whole family was trapped inside. They all passed."

"Except for Lex," I stated flatly without questioning. I didn't need to ask. I knew.

She nodded and continued to shed tears for the beautiful family our community had lost. I shed tears for the immense tragedy in what had stolen them away. He had actually done it. I might be the only one that knew, but I knew.

"What happened?" I asked numbly because I had nothing left to give emotionally.

"It looks as if it was a terrible accident. A gas leak at first. Everyone had been asphyxiated in their beds and then there was a fire. Poor little Lex had been hidden away in his treehouse out back. He woke up to the sound of an explosion in the basement. The darling boy had to stand by and watch his whole life on fire."

All the wind left me. I couldn't breathe. It was all too awful. How could he do that to his own family? I had thought it was going to be me, but he did it to his own family.

"It's all such a tragedy," she continued through sobs, "Just heartbreaking..."

She went on and on about "poor little Lex", but I had completely checked out at that point. I heard nothing she said. All I could hear was his little voice asking how a house catches on fire.

The rest of the school year after that day was a blur. I was just going through the motions. I could not understand how no one else had seen the truth in him. Then again, I had seen him in his manipulative games. I had been saying for the last 8 months that he was capable of something terrible and no one had believed me, yet I was still shocked myself.

Lex was never in my classroom again. With his parents and sister gone, he was sent to live with a grandmother in another state. I feared for her so intensely. It pained me to know she was now the sole family member to that little demon and she was being forced to read sensational headlines that blamed the whole devastation on her only son's negligence in ignoring the need for carbon monoxide detectors. It wasn't right or fair.

Over the years I've thought of her often and been tempted to Google her or Lex. I'm sure a simple search of either name would yield at least a couple of hits. I never doubted that trouble had followed his little life. I just could never bring myself to do it. I didn't want to face it. I wanted to erase his existence from my life and never think of him again. I would never be able to forget, of course, but I wouldn't give in to the temptation to cyberstalk either. That would have just pulled me right back in and I couldn't go there.

I just went on living my life. I began teaching at a new school. I mourned the death of my darling husband. I raised our sweet daughter. I built a new life as a single mother and a widow. We made it work, my Maggie and I. We have been happy. We have cried and laughed and yelled and hugged. It has been a beautiful journey with her and, over the years, I have only let the year I spent with Alexander Monroe be a minor blip on the radar of my life. A story I would tell someday when he finally got caught doing something else horrific without the ability to talk his way out of it. In recent years, I really hadn't thought of him at all. I never expected to have him hurled back into my mind so violently.

My Maggie had told me she was coming home from college to visit me for a weekend. I was over the moon excited and expected nothing but joy for her stay. When she walked in with a tall, blonde, blue-eyed young man I was taken a little aback because I had expected her to be alone, but it was when she spoke that I nearly died from complete shock.

"Mom, I want you to meet the love of my life, Lex Monroe!"

Baby Girl

"There are no secrets in life, just hidden truths that lie beneath the surface."
-Dexter Morgan

It has been 13 days since they buried their little girl. There is a hushed silence across their home. They both know what happened, but no one speaks it out loud. The gravity of it is just too much.

Before the funeral, everything moved so fast. There was no moment of stillness or quiet. Their home was filled with friends and community members sharing tears and trying to soothe the grief-stricken void of bereaved parents. What had happened to them was unthinkable. No parent should ever be forced to outlive their child. It was tragic, everyone who heard the news was certain. They had already been through so much as parents. Their baby had been born incomplete and never gained the ability to speak in her short 7 years of life. Her limbs had been twisted and tight with crippling disease. She had never been a child to the full degree one should be allowed. Her life was short and horribly disadvantaged, but she had always seemed so loved. Mommy and Daddy had been forced to tell her goodbye before she could ever truly say hello.

The paramedics had been crushed by the scene. They were the ones tasked with untangling the crumpled and broken body of a blonde-haired, green-eyed, little girl in a heap at the bottom of the cellar stairs. When they reached her, she was cold to the touch, her limbs stiff and unmoveable. Her white-blonde hair was stained with chunks of syrupy blood that had pooled around her. Her eyes were wide and looked like cold marbles sunken into her tiny face. Any hope for revival had long past before her accident had ever been discovered by her sobbing, inconsolable parents. Every set of eyes that touched the scene, worked through tears streaking their faces.

There had been a cat in the cellar recently, they said. She had wanted to pet it so badly, they said. They had lovingly tucked her into bed that night. They thought she was asleep, they said. How could this happen, they cried. She was our world, they sobbed. We just want her back, they lied. Lucky for Mommy and Daddy, the lie fell on accepting ears.

There would be no justice for their little girl because no one would ever believe it was them. The world of their shiny suburban lifestyle would never be able to see past the perfect picture frame positioned on the mantle. They would never see into the nightmare living in this luxury home. No one would ever see the cold hand pushing her into darkness on that cold, rainy night. The warm fireplace crackling in the living room was always enough to camouflage the cold, wicked truth.

But Mommy and Daddy know. They know what they did to their pretty princess. Daddy knows how many times he touched her in the darkness, how many times he made her cry with a lover's caress. Mommy knows how hateful and jealous she has always been of their imperfect daughter, how wickedly envious she is at Daddy's attraction to their broken offspring. She knows how gritty that hatred has grown in her gut, but Baby would never tell because she never learned how.

The smiles they paint on are never written in love. They have simply worn a perfect storybook cover on top of a horror story life. As long as it looks good to spectators, nevermind how ugly it is inside. They had shattered their princess long before pushing her down that dark stairway to a cold, damp death.

What they don't know is that even the earth itself can feel the unfair cruelty in their crime and Mother Earth is their baby's life-giver now. They took her out of this hateful world only sending her to a place of quiet and comfort down below the grass, six feet deep. Baby girl slumbers in her wooden box with the weight of the world holding her down, yet still more free than her life had been. She can finally stretch out her bones. Her muscles can relax from their disabled tense. Mother Earth is making Princess the body she has never had. She is growing strong and able. As each day passes and her skin dries like tissue paper, translucent and green over her little frame, she begins to stir in her tiny velvet-lined cocoon. Mother Earth has worked her magic to pry open this death box, and as the first little worm wriggles in and lands on Baby's lacy Sunday dress, her eyes fly open and she unleashes a bubble of giggles.

Her sweet smile reveals chipped and broken teeth barely managing to cling to rotting gums. Her shriveled fingers gently lift the squirming worm and drop it into her dry, crusted mouth. The wet squishing sound as she grinds it between her decaying teeth makes her giggle again. It feels like jello between her teeth, but it tastes like dirt and wet grass. She enjoys it down here in this little cradle of dirt, but she misses the sunshine on her skin.

Like a gruesomely beautiful butterfly being reborn, she just knows what to do and finally has the strength in her soul to do it. Mother Earth gives her the help she needs and loosens the graveyard dirt above the metamorphosis. Princess's need for oxygen has ceased to exist and she swims herself through the dirt, soil, and grass until she pops through like a budding spring flower. It is dark and foggy as her little hands push through the cemetery sod and free her from the grave. The moisture in the air clings to her now brown, muddied white lace. So strange that Mommy and Daddy would dress her in white for the afterlife when they both know they stole her innocence a long time ago.

She feels it again this night though, a childlike joy like firecrackers through her dead insides. She skips through the grass, playing her own private game of hide and seek between the gravestones. She releases delighted peals of laughter as she jumps through puddles like she has always wanted to. She throws handfuls of brown, orange, and yellow leaves into the air, relishing their cold feel as they rain back down on her. Her skin makes funny crinkling sounds like paper as she makes her way through deserted midnight streets in her small town. She can experience the world around her so much more clearly in death and it makes her smile. She smells the musty coolness of fall rains, garbage cans at the end of driveways, and, as she makes her way through the neighborhood she spent her life in, the smell of her favorite cookies. She remembers eating them only once, but will never forget the hot sweetness of cinnamon melting over her tongue. They tasted like the pictures of Christmas in Mommy's magazines. She loved them so much that Mommy never made them again after that one time.

On this night, it is like Mommy knows she is coming home and made them as a special surprise for her.

Following her nose to the yard she knows so well, she climbs the steep driveway one bone-cracking step at a time. She feels a soft nudge against her legs and softly sighs at the sight of Kitty rubbing against her. Silently, she lifts the moist ball of fur to her face and nuzzles her lovingly. Kitty is the only thing that really loved her in life and Mommy and Daddy had refused to let her into their warm, dry home. This gives Baby Girl a new kind of feeling she isn't used to. It makes her skin feel sticky hot and her stomach feel like rocks are tumbling around inside. It makes her face feel tight and a little like Mommy's used to look when she was mad. Is this mad? She knows sad, lonely, scared, hurt... but was this mad?

Tucking Kitty under her arm, she walks up to the bright windows of the house she is finally free of. Placing dirt-caked tips of rotten flesh up on the outside window ledge, she pulls herself up onto tiptoes to peer inside. Mommy and Daddy are laying on the couch together. They are talking to each other are smiling. They are enjoying their childless home and watching her favorite tv show. She had loved to watch it from the crack in her bedroom door before Daddy would come in to touch her. It was her favorite because it made Daddy happy and when Daddy was happy he just wanted to feel good, not to hurt her.

A raspy growl seeps from her chest remembering those moments and she feels that icky hot in her stomach again. Her dry and yellowed eyelids narrow around the shrivels orbs behind them. If she were still alive she would feel the sting of tears, but their absent now and that makes her anger grow intensely.

Her crunchy skin sounds now join the low rattle of her loose bones with each running step toward the cellar window behind the home. She had used this window so many times during life. When Mommy and Daddy would lock her in the basement, she would crawl up into this window ledge and slip out into the night. She was always too afraid to run away, but she loved to feel the cool grass on her skin before locking herself back into her prison. This window is where she first found Kitty too.

She gives Kitty a loving squeeze before letting her slip silently into the cool basement. Quiet as can be, Baby shimmies on her belly going feet first into the window. Slowly, she eases herself into the opening until her feet are as close to the floor as her tiny body will reach. As she lets go and crashes to the floor there is a loud, solid crack as her ankles give way to the weight of her corpse. Trying to stand upright now makes her crumple into a pile of her own decay. With the wild-eyed wonder of the child she never got to be, she stares down at the sharp angle of her useless ankles. Without hesitation and swift twist, she snaps the joint back to its natural position. Kitty rubs against her and she smiles her rotten smile. She now stands and walks toward the long staircase leading to her home. Pops and cracks echo in the open concrete room with every step. Pausing at the bottom of the stairs, she looks from the stained floor to the top step and remembers every moment of her final fall down those steps. She remembers every break, cut, and bruise. She remembers the blackout crack of her tiny skull hitting hard cement in an unforgiving thwack. More than anything she remembers Daddy telling her she could bring Kitty inside from the cellar, but finding Mommy waiting on the stairs instead. She remembers calling out to Mommy as her cold hand shoved against her Princess's chest, sending her into a freefall to the end. She remembers the last shred of her heart splinter to bits as Mommy and Daddy stood hand in hand watching her reach for them to save her as she fell.

That angry stomachache takes her over again now and makes her feel tingly all over. The putrid bile in her gut boils up her esophagus and drips from her lips as she begins dragging her fury up the creaking steps, knowing what brought her here tonight. Her rotting smile grows larger and larger as she gets closer and closer to the top.

Directly above her, Mommy and Daddy stiffen as they smell the wretched reek of death curling it's way through their home. They have been soaking up their joy in a childless home, but now share a look as a slow creaking rises up from the basement below them. They both pull themselves free of their lovely parentless evening to share a concerned look as they hear the distinct click and creak of the basement door slowly opening. The uneasy, queasy guilt surrounding that very door closes down on them like a vice. Silence descends again and then there is a soft meowing slipping in through the quiet.

Mommy and Daddy both relax and share a laugh over their silly uneasiness. Hand in hand, they rise from the couch and walk to find this furry visitor. Perhaps now that it's just the two of them, they'll invite Kitty in to stay. As they enter the kitchen they see this sweet ball of fur sitting in the crack of the basement door. They ooh and ahh over her petite size, but feel unsure of ever getting that awful smell off of her. She smells as it she has rolled in something long dead.

Hiding in the darkness of the corner behind her parents is the baby girl that only ever wanted them to love her. Her furious hate now bubbles over and out of her in a sinister laugh that brings Mommy and Daddy into a new reality. As they spin to find the source of the noise, Baby emerges from the darkness. Flesh is falling from her face in chunks revealing the bone beneath. The half-eaten worm has worked its way through her sinus cavity to seek out escape through her nostril now. She is grotesque and they cty out in horror of what they created. She races toward them, crooked and broken limbs outstretched at unnatural angles and forces them toward the open basement door.

"Mommy! Daddy! I've come back to play," she trills in an unnervingly sweet refrain.

Those are the first words Baby Girl has ever spoken to Mommy and Daddy. How fitting that they would also be the last words Mommy and Daddy ever get to hear.

Dark Water

"Sink or swim."
-William Shakespeare

Skin, tight and pink from the warm summer sun. Eyes red and burning from too much cheap beer and last night's bonfire. Hair somehow oily and dry all at the same time from days and days spent in the lake's gritty water. Thoughts churning restlessly, obsessed with last night's campfire stories.

I always revel in the mystery and intrigue held by this beautiful place.

Lake life is my very favorite thing in this whole wide world and this lake is where I have grown up. Every single summer since birth I have been at this lake. It feels like home. It's really the only place that I have ever really felt like

I belong. I don't fit anywhere else in this world. I like it here where things are slow and all about the Earth. That is the life I was meant to live and I often wonder if I was born to the wrong time. I should have lived when all I needed was a little cabin in the middle of nowhere, where I would grow my own food and spend endless days barefoot enjoying the sunshine through the trees. I just want eternal summertime.

This will likely be the last summer I have to spend freely lounging with my friends from June all the way through August. I will start college in the fall and then real life begins. It's such a strange and bittersweet phase of life. So ready for the freedom of adulthood, but so not ready to let go of the entirely different kind of freedom that childhood offers. Maybe I should be a teacher and keep my carefree summers forever. Definitely, something to think about.

I stretch out my body across the slick sleeping bag I'm cocooned in and feel all my muscles ache with fatigue. It is the stiff throb you can only get from sleeping on the ground. I find it absolutely delightful and smile through my sleepiness.

Our campsite is still silent and I am the first from our little tribe of misfits that is awake, as always. These are my favorite moments of the day. The birds are singing their songs of good morning, but the rest of the world is calm and still.

I grab one of my coffee drinks from the cooler and walk across the sharp rocks of the shore to the edge of the water. I let the drinks sticky, sweet thickness fill my body with a caffeinated jolt as the cool water washes up onto my manicured toes. I stare towards the cove across the water, where the bottom of the lake seems nonexistent beneath the dark water. No one swims there. People have drowned there. Too many people for anyone to feel like it is a safe place. No bodies are ever found after they swim in that cove. They just sort of disappear right there in that inky dark water. It is like a life-sucking vortex that you just can't outswim.

I've always been inexplicably drawn to that exact spot. Yet another thing that makes me strange and unusual. I don't know why or how... I just know that I feel its pull like a magnet drawing me in. It's been like that as long as I can remember. My parents were constantly chasing me back to the safety of the roped-off swimming area even when I was barely swimming at all. So many times I would swim to the very farthest edge of the swimming area and drape my body over the buoyed ropes that caged me in. I would hang there all day just looking to the cove I was forbidden to be in.

I have always just been hoping if I watch long enough I might catch another glimpse. It's only ever happened one time before, but I have never forgotten her.

At first, I just noticed a rippling wave across the top of still water. It was a smooth and languid movement that seemed to materialize out of nothing. I thought it was a fish rolling against the surface of the water, but on second thought it just seemed different somehow. I kept watching, mesmerized by the graceful ripples. I could have sworn for just a moment that I saw delicate feminine fingers break the surface in a kind of ballerina movement. I couldn't have torn my eyes away if I had been forced and my breathing slowed to nearly nothing. The sounds of the others behind me splashing and yelling in the water faded to near silence as my focus zeroed in on the cove and the cove alone. That's when I saw her. Just barely peeking out above the water was a pair of emerald green eyes that locked with mine for the briefest moment and then she was gone with a flash of red hair and the tiniest little splash. Not a single day has gone by since that I haven't thought of her. She has filled my dreams and my days for all these years.

51

I was ten when I first saw her and I felt a little touch of magic in the moment we shared. As I have gotten older that magic sparkle has grown into something so much more. I feel something deeper within me when I think of her now. It is a heat that makes my skin flush and my groin ache. I have always wanted to reach out and touch her, but now I want her to touch me too. The mere thought makes me shiver.

Looking over my shoulder now, I see that everyone at our campsite is still sleeping like the dead. I slip off my coverup and walk into the water. My swimsuit, crisp from days of dried water, quickly soaks us the wake as I wade in further and further. The whole time I keep my eyes riveted to the dark cove as I make my way across. After a few moments of stumbling across the sharp, rocky lake bottom, I feel it drop out from under me and my body begins to bob in the water. I stretch out my arms and relish the feeling of cool water flowing over my skin as I swim faster and faster across the calm morning lake. I stop and tread water just outside the cove and watch it's churning ripples.

It feels so surreal. Like science fiction. It sparks something in me, always has, and it draws me in like a moth to the flame. I understand that it might consume me, but I can't help but chase it anyway.

Without thought, I dive down into the water and paddle myself to the very middle of that forbidden zone for the first time ever. I have finally done this thing that I'm not supposed to and it fills me with rebellious glee. I let myself float along in the black as night water and feel her magic wrap itself around me like a warm blanket. I feel like this spot has been waiting for me to be here and now we are both complete. I feel her warmth fill me up just as a cold touch wraps itself around my foot and leg.

Before I even know what is happening, my body is

plunging deeper and deeper into the frigid depths. The expanding darkness feels crushing as the light from the surface grows dimmer, but I don't panic. I just hold my breath to the best of my ability and wait. I knew what I was getting myself into with this little venture.

I seem to be still now and the hard pull on my leg has morphed into a tight hold anchoring me to the spot instead. I can see nothing but green tinted blackness around me as I blink through the sting of dirty water against my eyes. I can feel myself being watched. Slowly from the darkness I can see a figure begin to take shape. At first a cloudy silhouette then slowly a porcelain pale face with eyes so green they nearly glow. She comes closer still and I can see her whole self.

She is beautiful.

Her hair is a deep auburn red flowing around her in watery crown of fire. Her nose and cheeks are covered in a spattering of freckles. Her lips are full and plump, begging to be kissed. Her body is bare and curved in the most seductive ways. The wide curve of her hips slides down into a lower half that is not human. As she draws closer and closer to me I can see a tangle of tentacles swirling around me. They are wrapping themselves around me and pulling me to her. Nose to nose now, being this close rattles my serene resolve and I start to take a deep breath only to feel the sting of water pouring down my throat and into my lungs. This is the first moment I have felt even a slight pang of panic and my face betrays the secret. This beautiful woman of the lake sees it and smoothes her hand through my hair in a calming gesture. She pulls my mouth towards hers and our lips connect. I can feel her forcing air into my body.

The relief is immediate and makes me feel full and whole again. She pulls away and gives me a sweet smile when she sees that the fear has left my face. For a long moment we just float here, frozen with our eyes locked on one another. She is even more than I imagined.

Eventually, she brings her lips back to mine again, but this time they share a mutual embrace, even parting enough so our tongues can brush one another. The kiss is somehow tender and aggressive all at once. It is so intense that I can feel it all the way to my toes and I am confident that if I was standing on solid ground I would be weak in the knees. Even the best kiss I have ever had up until this moment is no comparison for this. Being connected to her in this way seems so totally rooted in my DNA that I can't imagine a time before her. I feel fireworks explode within me, giving life to parts of my soul that have never existed before. We both greedily deepen our embrace, tangling our fingers in each others flowing hair around us. My brain begins a chant:

I am hers and she is mine.

I am hers and she is mine.

I am hers and she is mine.

I don't know how I know it. I just feel it inside. I was meant for her. I think, now that the lightbulb has gone off for me, that I have always known that since the first time I caught a glimpse of her.

We break our kiss, she places her forehead against mine, and I know that she has known it since that day as well. I know because she is telling me through her touch. With our minds this close, her intimate gesture is giving me the ability to see the world through her eyes. I see the day she peeked at me through the bright daylight of a summer day shining through the protection of her waves. I can feel how her heartbeat thrummed like a hummingbird's the moment our eyes met. She shows me how she has so often been drawn to the unattainable shore just as I have been drawn to her cove.

She breaks the contact between our consciousness to breathe another burst of air into my lungs. I am thankful for the oxygen that instantly dulls the ache in my chest, but I am also suddenly cold in the absence of her thoughts. She pulls away again and stares at me intently. I blink my eyes against the harsh water and nod in answer to her silent question. Yes, I want to know more. Yes, please tell me more. She smiles, kisses my forehead, and then pushes memories into me once again.

At first, I don't see anything, but I feel an edge of hesitation and worry. I try to tell her with my own mind that she should never fear to tell me anything and it must work because fuzzy images of her life begin to take shape again.

I don't understand what I'm seeing. I focus on the images in my head and see bodies tangled in the weeds sprouting from the lake floor. They are young and old, men and women. I recognize them from all the years of memorials to local drowning victims.

One by one, I see flashes of my love pulling these victims down to their watery graves. I see her putting her mouth to theirs and sucking the life force out of them in the reverse of how she has just breathed life into me. I am watching it all happen from the most recent one to the very first. With each step back in time and each victim restored to life before death, she becomes less and less human. Her beautiful body fades to a sickly green before morphing completely into a creature of the sea, what looks like an octopus tangled in the lake weeds that hold her to this cove, like organic restraints.

She leans away from me now. Her face is sorrowful and unsure. She wants to know if I understand. She takes the souls of others to give herself one. The more she takes the closer she becomes to being something closer to human. She wants to walk the earth. It is all she has ever wanted.

I understand the despicable gravity of this, but still, I wonder to myself, how close is she? How many more lives would it take? The idea is absurd, yet… I want to give myself for her. I would trade life for her. I don't even know why.

I pull her into a crushing embrace so firm that we nearly melt into one being. I need her to understand that I know what I need to do so she can be whole and human again. That is what I want most of all. I just want to make her feel whole again. Every single soul on this earth deserves that. I need to know I helped her escape this aquatic prison.

We share another long look before she gives me one more deep breath and releases her hold on me. The air she pumped into me seems to lift me upwards more quickly than I imagined it would. I let it carry me toward the sky as I watch my fire-haired beauty fade into the darkness below me. As she completely disappears into the black I begin kicking my feet and swimming toward the glowing surface. I pop up out of the water and gasp for the humid air around me. I blink frantically and look around me in every direction. Did that really just happen?

Yes. I can still feel the heat of her lips on mine.

She has sent me back to my world unlike all the others that have ever shared in her space, but I know I will go back. I want to be a part of her and I want her to be a part of me. I have always felt the draw of her, but now I feel as though I have tasted her sweet heroin for the first time. What has always been just a passing wince of want is now a powerful hunger of need.

I am hers and she is mine.

I am hers and she is mine.

I want to be one with her. I want to breathe in the dark water until I have become like her.

I am hers and she is mine.

It's like she is inside me already. I can feel my desire

56

for her swimming its way through my veins. The need now pounds in my chest with my anxious breaths.

I am hers.

Without a second thought, I release as much oxygen as possible and dive back down into the depths.

She is mine.

I propel myself back down into the dark until I can see her green eyes shining at me through the murky depth. She is smiling at me as I return to her. Being in her presence again, I feel palpable relief in my soul and rejoice as she embraces me.

Looking into her face and feeling the burning ache of oxygen deprivation in lungs, I realize what has just happened.

I am hers.

I am hers.

I am hers.

Just like all those before me, I have become the next face on the missing flyers. I will be forever immortalized as a victim to this lake. My life will be regarded as all the others, a brief and tragic story to be told around the campfire.

As I feel my lungs shrinking in their need to breathe again, I stare into her perfect face and smile.

Just like all the others, I will let her take me just to feel the ambrosia of her kiss again. Heavenly, sinful, sweet, and worth every last moment of dark.

You Should Ride the Carousel

"The only certainty about following the crowd is that you will get there together."
-Mychal Wynn

W. D. Pelley's Grand Carnival was being billed as "the hottest ticket in town for the lowest price around". This was the first time anyone had ever heard of it before, but the near-constant local advertising promised an experience unlike any other for "low, low price of fifty cents a person", keeping with the vintage vibes being promised. The overwhelmingly broad marketing campaign had ensured that every single person within 50 miles was planning to attend. It was the place to be.

Mallory had begged to go the second she heard their rockabilly radio spot. It had been designed to reel her in just like it had and Jordan rolled his eyes but immediately agreed. That girl was the one he was going to spend his life with. He loved her in ways he never knew were possible. She could ask him to go to the moon and he would agree.

She gushed about it for weeks leading up to the big day and it had become a joke to Jordan. Her over the top excitement made him shake his head and laugh. Nothing about the 1950's sounded appealing to him, but by the time the opening day came, Mallory had him pumped and ready to go too.

Pulling into the parking lot, they were directed to a spot by men dressed in red and white striped jackets with bow ties. Their heads proudly wore straw hats and they directed drivers with their long wooden canes. This place really seemed to know how to play up a gimmick. Mallory squealed with delight at the ridiculous authenticity and flashed Jordan her best smile.

Approaching the ticket booth was like walking even further into a time warp. A tall fence reached toward the sky, blocking out the excitement inside, but screaming fun with it's bold red, yellow, and white stripes. The line was miles long but seemed to be moving pretty quickly. It seemed astonishing that this many people could fit inside those fenced-in walls.

As they made it to the front of the line, the woman in the ticket booth was so beyond stereotypical white, suburban 1950, it was almost comical. Her long, red fingernails reached out to exchange cash for little blue tickets that were stamped, "Admit One" and her smile seemed to stretch unnaturally wide across her face to reveal bright white shining teeth. She was decked out in a vintage dress that seemed to float around her but didn't distract from her tornado of springy curls swirled on top of her head in a tremendous bouffant hairstyle.

Not to be overdone by its greeter, the carnival erupted with sounds from behind the tall striped wall. The whooshing sound of rides flying across metal tracks meshed with the giggles and screams of too many people to count. Combine all that with the sound of early rock and roll blaring from enormous speakers and it was almost overwhelming.

Jordan stared around himself in absolute awe of what he was seeing. Mallory gazed at it all with love. He wasn't sure he wanted to know what was on the other side of that towering wall, but she wanted to touch, taste, and experience it all. He smiled and laughed a little under his breath at her round sparkling eyes and the supreme joy she showed over the whole spectacle. He honestly felt no nostalgia for a decade long gone and full of serious ugliness, but for her, he would pretend to love anything.

"How many," twanged the caricature of a woman in the ticket booth.

"Two please," he requested politely to the unmoving smile in front of him.

"Oh, you two are together," she asked looking from Jordan to Mallory and back again.

Jordan hesitated as he glanced down at Mallory's hand clearly threaded through his own, "Um… yes, ma'am," and handed over his money.

The woman's unwavering smile was robotic and almost eerie, but she handed over the tickets saying, "You should ride the carousel."

With an awkward nod, Jordan followed his love's tug toward the entrance. As they approached the ticket taker, he notices another unwavering smile. This guy is a Danny Zuko wannabe dressed in cuffed blue Levi's, a white t-shirt, and a worn leather jacket.

He gives Mallory a wholesome megawatt smile, but darts his eyes at Jordan and asks, "Is this boy bothering you?"

The couple shares a bemused look and laugh as they raise their still clasped hands in the air. She replies, "No! He's my boyfriend!"

"Oh, good for you I guess," he says with a shrug, still smiling as he takes their tickets and waves them through a curtain hiding the main attraction. They glance back at him as he yells, "You should ride the carousel!"

This whole experience is so alien to Jordan thus far and he is not yet a fan. The scene is an assault on the senses. Bright lights of every color flash and gleam everywhere around them. The smell of popcorn and cotton candy mingle with sweat and fried greasiness. The blaring speakers pound out classic songs over the shouts and laughter of riders while games send out dings, whirs, and groans for every win and loss. More men in striped coats coax passersby to see their attraction while onlookers seem to be in the same state of awe as Mallory.

"What first, babe," Jordan asks as he leans in to kiss her cheek and bring her back to reality.

Batting her eyelashes at him as she snakes her arm around his waist, "Win me a prize, lover?"

The pair make their way to the Hammer of Strength. It is the same game everyone has seen at every carnival since the beginning of carnivals. Take the hammer, slam it down as hard as you can, and watch as the little metal slider tries to reach the big shiny bell at the top.

"Step right up ladies and gents! Test your strength and win a prize," a mustached strong man blasts to the crowd. Glancing down at the couple now he continues, "I bet this strapping boy can win a prize for the lady," with that same overstretched smile as the others.

Something in the way the man calls him "boy" rubs Jordan the wrong way, but he lets it roll off of him with a shrug of the shoulders.

"Show them how it's down stud," Mallory says as she pushes him forward with a firm slap on the butt.

He laughs, "You just watch and learn sweetheart," and gives her his cheesiest wink.

The muscle man with his robotic smile and perfect teeth hands Jordan the hammer with unblinking eyes. Their cold blankness gives Jordan an ache in the pit of his stomach. It is like this man is missing something inside him. That spark that makes us human is missing from his eyes. Jordan doesn't break eye contact as he reaches for the hammer. For the briefest moment he fears the man may bash his head in with the hammer instead. The image of his own body on the ground with his skull leaking all of his brain matter on the dirty concrete flashes through his mind and he flinches.

"What's the matter boy, are you one of those sissy boys," asks the man with the wicked smile.

Jordan grabs the hammer with a yank and readies himself to play as the man laughs behind him. Channeling all of his frustration with this strange place into a splintering whack, he slams the hammer down onto the rubber pad. With a whirring crash the metal slider sails to the top and chimes the winner bell with a hard strike.

"Winner, winner! Chicken dinner," the mustached man exclaims to passersby. Leaning down toward Jordan and widening his smile even more, if that's possible, he finishes with a quiet whisper, "Give the lady her prize, boy."

Jordan snatches the stuffed elephant from the man and rolls his eyes. He tosses the toy to his love and happily walks away from the strong man.

"Hey folks," the strong man yells after them, "You should ride the carousel."

Mallory, seemingly unaware of all the weirdness around them, stands on her tiptoes to kiss Jordan's lips. His tense shoulders loosen some at this gesture, but he still officially hates everything about this place. He can't even entirely put his finger on what it is that rubs him the wrong way, but something here just isn't right.

"I cannot possibly be the only one here that thinks this is the creepiest, strangest, most ridiculous place I've ever been…" Jordan speaks to the petite brunette on his arm.

With a giggle she pulls herself into his side, "I think it's quirky and fun. At least it's something different."

"I have been called 'boy' at least five times in the few minutes that we have been here. Those painted on smiles are fucking scary. That last dude was straight-up crazy. This whole thing is straight-up crazy."

"It's just harmless fun! Don't read so much into it, babe," Mallory pleads with a pout. "What harm could it do to just play along for a while?"

Jordan puts on his own version of the overstretched smile and talks through gritted teeth, "You don't even think the carousel sounds weird?"

Mallory laughs steadily now as they continue a leisurely stroll down the fairway, "Okay, okay… that is a little weird, but you know what I think?"

"Please tell, oh wise one," he says with a cocked brow.

"It must be a really badass carousel."

He laughs at this now and they come to an agreement. He promises to ride the carousel with her if she agrees to let him leave a one-star google review when they leave.

The rest of their evening continues along the same lines. Everything seems delightful to sweet Mallory, weird and unsettling to Jordan. He continues to let her have her fun as he counts down the minutes to when they can leave.

They order corndogs and fresh-squeezed lemonade

from an elderly couple dressed like a past their prime vaudeville act, but still wearing that horror movie smile. Of course, as they part ways with the couple they hear, "You should ride the carousel!"

They ride a seven-story roller coaster that Jordan is sure actually came directly from circa 1952 and would never in a million years pass current safety standards. It is being run by a barbershop quartet with teeth exposed as they sing farewell to riders with, "You should ride the carousel," in perfect harmony.

They even fumble their way through the house of mirrors that has an odd odor of gunpowder inside it. As they make their way through to the final hallway leading to the glowing exit, there is a sparkling sign above the door. In giant, bold, jolly letters it says, "You should ride the carousel!". The glittering words reflect off of every wall and surface around them, forcing the sentiment in their faces from a thousand shining angles.

The longer they stay, the louder and more often they begin to hear it all around them. It is becoming a crushing weight piling itself on top of them and beating them down. Finally, enough is enough and the pair are ready to escape to their own quiet home, but not until after that carousel ride. With all that hype, there is no way they are leaving this crazy place without their carousel ride. Someday they plan to tell this story and the carousel details are a must.

Off on their mission they go, to find this special ride that has somehow remained elusively hidden from sight all night. They are certain they have seen everything except this mysterious main attraction. Then, suddenly, it's just there. It is almost like their search brought it to life.

Before them is a giant blue and silver striped tent hovering against the horizon. It seems to glow in a way that defies understanding, like the fabric itself is made from the faint glow of a million fireflies. How had they ever missed this beautiful thing before them? Now that it is in their sight, they can't look away. Without even realizing it, they walk toward its glow and let the heavy canvas flaps settle behind them. Inside this big top tent is warm and welcoming like a womb. It feels like a warm embrace.

"This place is magic," Mallory softly voices beside him.

Jordan has no words to respond as his eyes settle on the magnificent structure in the middle of the tent. Standing high above them are three stories of intricately carved wood and delicate paint strokes. Its proportions are beyond belief. It is the most magnificently tremendous thing they have ever seen. The carousel.

Resonating all around it is that same luminescent glow, but it also has an almost sheer transparency. Like fog, it grabs hold of every spark of white, yellow, pink, and blue lighting around the whole room. Without a doubt, this is the finest attraction ever erected for any carnival.

The line to ride is long and winds its way around the entire tent. Each person waiting their turn stands silent staring up at the beautiful extravagance before them. No one complains about their wait or their tired feet. There is no reason to speak. They all share mutual awe that words cannot express.

The line of silent onlookers funnels forward as the ride begins accepting a new set of riders. Half the waiting crowd is swallowed up by the massive carousel and the rest watch as the lucky ones claims their place riding atop fantastical creatures that look so amazingly real that it's hard to believe they aren't. This is truly one of the most spectacular experiences these carnival-goers will ever witness.

As all the seats fill, the riders giggling and whispering, a soft velvet curtain slowly falls around all three levels. The black cloth suffocates out all sights and sounds behind it and the crowd still waiting their turn moans in collective disappointment. Jordan and Mallory find themselves among the group of impatient waiters craning their necks to try and steal just one more glimpse inside.

Jordan knows in the back of his mind that this is over the top and bizarre. He feels like this whole scene is too much and he wants to laugh at it with his love. He wants to lean down to whisper a snide remark in her ear and then watch her face light up with a shared giggle, but he can't do that. He can't control any of what he is doing right now. Even his seemingly genuine reactions are some kind of forced thing that he has no control over. He is still in there somewhere, but he isn't as strong as the power of the room drawing him into its absurd grandiosity. No matter how loudly his rational consciousness screams out, it cannot be heard over the magic of the carousel before him.

As it begins to spin in front of them, light bubbling music spills into the tent. The music spreads through the line causing all those waiting to sway rhythmically together with the coursing beat. Jordan feels himself join this gentle back and forth, but doesn't know why. What is happening?

Within less than a minute, or maybe a few hours... Jordan can't really distinguish time anymore, the carousel comes to a stop. They all rise up on tiptoes to try and catch a view inside again. For several moments they stand perfectly still with the music still softly lilting through the tent. After an excruciating wait, the velvet curtains rise up and reveal an again empty carousel. Excitement spreads through the crowd as their turn approaches.

Soon they're all climbing aboard and silently filing into their own spot on top of magical creatures that seem to be made just for them.

Jordan watches as Mallory climbs onto a dark, deep

purple unicorn. Its coat shimmers like jewels and it is so sculpted with muscles that it looks as if it could run away or burst through its own skin. Sitting on it bareback, Mallory looks like a queen. Majestic and regal.

Jordan mounts a giant phoenix with flames seeming to flow from its body. It feels uncomfortably hot against his skin and almost alive. It seems to have a light sheen of sweat across its feathered exterior. Its flesh seems to give way to the pressure and weight of Jordan's body on it. Squeezing his thighs down around it, Jordan thinks he can almost feel it breathing beneath him. He leans down and lays his whole body against the creature, swearing the mechanical tick he hears could almost be a heartbeat. As he closes his eyes and breathes in its sharp animalistic mustiness, Jordan hears a soft rustling of fabric.

Opening his eyes now, he sees the thick velvet curtain gliding down around them and closing them in a shroud of darkness that suddenly sucks out all of the warmth and comfort from their world. Trapped now in this cold blackness, a little bit of their former consciousness snaps back into place with a jolt. Suddenly a heavy tension settles over all of them.

"Jordan," Mallory calls from beside him with tears in her voice, "What is happening?"

Low whispers and murmurs begin to rise around them. There is a collective confusion that begins morphing into panic as the creatures beneath them begin to writhe and move. The air is now filled with the sounds of hisses, moans, and growls on top of shrieks, screams, and moans. The world they find themselves in now is one they could never understand no matter how hard they may try and it is so very frightening.

The momentum of the spinning carousel now picks up more and more speed. As the centrifugal force pulls and tugs at the riders, bright white lights begin to flash at near strobe light speed. It gives first light to all the horrifying things happening around them. There is blood. There are body parts. The ones they boarded the ride with are being slaughtered before their eyes and it seems only a matter of time before each rider will be next. Each flash of bright white shows a glimpse of some monster coming at them to try and eat them alive. In the background is the sound of laughter. Like a laugh track from an old sitcom, their deaths seem to be tonight's entertainment.

Finally, a serpent still carrying its long-dead rider's headless corpse, latches onto Jordan. It pulls him from his mounted seat as the phoenix he had been clinging to flies across the aisle and snips the guts out of a fellow rider with its razor-sharp beak. The serpent wraps itself around Jordan's body, crushing him alive one bone at a time. As he lays with his cheek pressed against the ground he sees Mallory on the ground with him. Her back is flat against the metal floor and blood is pooled under her head, soaking her hair and making it shimmer in the flashing lights. Her eyes are staring blankly and hold no evidence of the sparkling girl that once stared at him through those brown eyes. He tries to reach out and touch her, but just as his fingertips brush against her porcelain skin the serpent crashes its giant fangs into Jordan's head, collapsing it like a popped balloon.

That was the last moment Jordan as the world had known him ever existed. Everything went black in that instant it would never shine on his world again.

Meanwhile, outside of the small compartment that was Jordan's conscious mind, his body remained sitting upon that golden phoenix, upright and completely safe. As did his love, sweet Mallory, and all the other riders that day. Not all of them had seen the same death for themselves, but they had all seen something that pointed to the death of who they once were. Their bodies remained untouched but they were gone. They had been slaughtered in the mind. They were the others now.

As the carousel comes to a stop each rider stands and walks out single-file through an exit. As they each pass through this gateway to their community, their enormous ear-to-ear smiles stretch their skin tight as one by one they all chant, "You should ride the carousel." They walk out into the night following all the other others that had been born today. They walk out into the world and destroy it until everyone who wasn't like them is gone.

It is a total reset of the world carried out by a dying population. Anyone who isn't like them is turned into them or devoured. Their life is now to walk the earth telling others what had once been said to them with old-fashioned, American as apple pie smiles.

You should ride the carousel.

Ghosts of Ex Lovers Past

"Sooner or later, everyone sits down to a banquet of consequences."
-Robert Louis Stevenson

James Ellison was not a good man.

He was often assumed to be. It was an easy assumption to make. He showed up to church every Sunday. He lent a hand to help those in the community. He was friendly and loved to share a laugh over coffee. He did all the things one is supposed to do to gain the reputation of a good, upstanding man, but it was never real.

He was a con man of the most predatory type. He knew how to play all the right games in all the right ways and if he lost anyway, he would steal whatever he felt entitled to. He had made a career of it. Everywhere he drove that big rig, he left behind a string of wronged, cheated, and broken, from one side of the country to the other.

But that was in his prime.

He is old now, grey and feeble with no hope for redemption. His life will end tonight and he will face death alone because that is the fate he created for himself.

Of course, though, he doesn't know he is going to die tonight. He doesn't even realize he's alone. How could he? He is a newlywed, after all. He and lovely wife number eight seem quite charmed with one another, or at least until her money runs out.

Little does he know, he has met his match with this one. That delicious dinner she has been cooking him every night is slowly killing him from the inside out and he is blissfully unaware of the whole treachery.

He is sure he just hasn't been feeling well. That is an unavoidable part of aging and he isn't in the best of health anyway. Before he goes to bed every night he just feels tired and nauseous. Sometimes his head hurts and lately it's been getting harder to breathe sometimes. Going to the bathroom has gotten harder to, like his bladder has just dried up. All his insides just don't want to work quite right, but his new wife has been taking sweet care of him. He smiles thinking of her; thinking this one might be different. She'll help him through this spell of sickness and he will be just fine.

She knows different though. Just a few dribbles of antifreeze in each evening's meal is sufficient. It is enough to send him stumbling sickly to the bedroom each night until he finally succumbs to the angry crystals now terrorizing his kidneys. Eileen knows they have been married long enough now and he is in poor enough health on his own that no one will bat an eye when the old bastard keels over from kidney failure. He has no family to call his own anymore, they hate him too, so she will be the sole inheritor of his goodies pilfered from all the marriages before her. She will play the mournful wife for a while and then she can enjoy the last of her own days without a worry or a care in the world.

As each night has passed he has grown more and more ill, always peaking in his discomfort after dinner. He is fairly incoherent tonight and she smiles sweetly as she kisses her husband goodnight for what will be the last time.

Deep down inside of his waning consciousness, he is still clueless about what is happening but he thinks he can see a face coming into focus above him. James is sure it must be his lovely wife. You know, he actually might really like this one.

Funny how fate works out that way.

As the face draws closer, he instead sees the kind eyes of Aggie, the woman he married when he was only 19 years old. She had been his first wife, so beautiful and so naive. She had waited on him hand and foot for the whole year they were married. Even on the nights he knocked around a bit, she had wanted nothing more than to please him and he had loved every minute of it. Unfortunately, he had also loved the minutes he spent with the other ladies in town, her sister included.

As her face fades from his mind it seems to be replaced with Joanna, the 16-year-old girl he had met when he was 38. She had been such a looker. She definitely had daddy issues and he used those to lure her in like a predator. Using her had been one of the greatest times in his life, but when she got pregnant he had to pretend he didn't know who she was. He couldn't end up tied down to all that mess. Besides, having a baby would ruin her looks and he had heard rumors that she got into drugs anyway.

She faded away as well and he began to see Morgan before him. He had married her after he found out she had received a settlement from her long-deceased husband's accidental death. She was rich overnight and terribly lonely.

She had just wanted companionship and he had gladly provided it. Until he had successfully spent all of her money, that is. He drug their divorce out so long that the stress of it all put her in an early grave.

The next face in his view becomes is his baby sister, Sherry. She was a beautiful girl from the day she was born, but he had not thoroughly enjoyed her until she got old enough to look like a woman. He had enjoyed her so very much after that. She felt so good that he'd happily have her again today if she hadn't slit her own wrists at 22.

This face now morphs into Alice, the wife he actually kept around for a few years. Alice had never been of much interest to him in the bedroom, but he did give her 3 children to make up for all the abuse she took from him when he was drunk. She had been the local pastor's daughter and he really needed that support to pull off a scam that he was running through the church. Once people started getting suspicious, he dropped Alice and walked away like their family had never existed. He doesn't even know if those kids are still around.

Betsy's face is before him now. Betsy had been the free-spirited flower child that ran away with him after a whirlwind summer romance. He had messed up and said "I love you" to that one. He only said it to see what she would let him do to her for love. She had taken that as permission to climb up in his truck and leave town with him. He had found the first scumbag infested motel he could and left her stranded for dead with a junkie who had a bad reputation.

There was Cynthia, the hooker he raped and left in a ditch.

Then Wilma, the single mom that had sucked him off before he molested her daughter.

Gail, the barmaid he'd beaten unconscious when she refused to serve him another drink.

Susan, the waitress he assaulted and then stole checks from.

Dorothy, the housekeeper he raped on his way to check out of another seedy motel.

This changing of faces grows faster now and James is afraid. He doesn't understand what is happening. Why have all these visions of the past come to haunt him? The room has become filled with a wicked energy that buzzes in his ears. The sound becomes more and more intense with every passing moment. He may go crazy, he thinks, but he never once comes to realize, this is death.

Jane.

Sadie.

Linda.

Rebecca.

Gloria.

One after another, the faces loom over this old, tired, and dying man. He feels a weight crushing his chest as they all fill the space around him.

Sherry.

Mona.

Renee.

His heartbeat feels like it may have forgotten to keep a steady beat. His breath feels trapped inside him.

Maria.

Zelda.

Corrine.

He feels claustrophobic in this room of women he has wronged and they all stare him down as he has trouble deciphering where he is. The pounding in his chest thuds harder, pinning him to his bed as the women come into perfect clarity surrounding him. A silence descends over the room and James can see nothing but their faces, now understanding these are the faces of the sins he will be judged by. The true nature of his fate now collapses upon him causing tears to drench his feverish face. He reeks of fear or maybe it's just piss, as the warm liquid floods the mattress beneath him. He tries to scream out to his new love and beg for her rescue, but the cold weight of death that she placed on him is too much for him to overcome.

As he takes each last breath on this earth, the women that he shattered close in on him in a cluster of anger. Each labored beat of his black heart draws his victims closer to retribution. As they now growl and hiss their need to destroy him, he prays for sweet death.

His prayers are answered and his body releases his soul into the next realm with the final expiring tick of his faulty heart. The other side of the veil welcomes him to his final place of residence and his victims rejoice in being there to greet him.

Finally, death was able to deliver him what he deserves and their wrath is forever his hell.

Hell Hole

"And all the while I thought I was drowning, I was actually the one holding my head under water."
-Maris Crane

I don't get a lot of days off work to sit in the woods. I had to beg, borrow, and bargain to get this one, but I needed it. I even picked the perfect rainy day, yet here I am walking back to my truck without a god damn bird. Without even seeing a single god damn bird. Frustrated doesn't even begin to cover the mood I'm in.

This spring just started and already I want a do-over. My life is a mess. I work all the fucking time just to make not shit. I just got left at the altar by my girlfriend of the last seven years. Now I can't even shoot a turkey on the only day off I'll have all season and, as I look up seeing nothing familiar, I might be lost to top it all off.

I've been so up here in my own head that I stopped looking for the reflective trail markers I left along the path to my blind. I was in a hurry when I did it a few weeks ago and I've only been here on this chunk of public land a couple of times, but I know I put up enough and I am positive I have never seen this part of the woods before. I sigh and drag my hands down across my face in exasperation then pull out my cell phone to look up my current location. It's dead because of course it is.

Thankfully I carry a handheld satellite GPS in my backpack. I sling my bag off my shoulder and drop it to the ground, wanting to throw it across the woods instead but knowing better. As I squat down to dig out my GPS, I lose my footing as the ground seems to give way under my weight. As I fall, I fully expect my back to hit the ground with a thud, giving me an excuse to cuss and remind myself what a total dumbass I am, but it seems like time has come to a complete stop. I just seem to keep falling.

I see my bag fly through the air away from me as my body instinctively flails while reaching for anything that might keep me from sinking any further from the ground I thought I was firmly planted on. There just seems to be nothing within reach and I start to feel like I'm being sucked down into hell as blackness begins to encircle everything in my vision. Is that what this is? Am I dead and being sent to hell where I belong? Did I have a heart attack right here in these woods? Or get shot by a stray bullet from a luckier hunter than I?

Just when I think I will never stop my descent and the light from the world I was just occupying has become a small glowing circle above me, my back slams against a hard and cold surface submerged under about two inches of frigid water. The impact paired with the icy cold steal my breath away for a long moment. The pain is so intense that I actually can't breathe.

I finally suck a deep, gasping breath into my aching lungs only to feel the initial shock of pain hit me all over again. Just breathing hurts. Just existing hurts across every single part of my body. Even my bones seem to be screaming out in agony deep inside my frame. Whatever that impact was, it just rattled everything in me. As my senses slowly seem to come back to me I begin feeling things beyond pain as well. There is cold wetness soaking through my layers of camo. So much for weatherproof…

My ability to process what I am seeing seems to be coming back too. Everything around me seems black and I can't see anything tangible, but that is still better than the white, glowing flash of having all sense knocked out of me. Is this the void? Have I died and gone to the in-between of purgatory? No, I hurt too much to be dead and my eyes are beginning to adjust to the darkness around me.

I look straight up and squint into the circle of light above my head. My neck aches and raindrops pelt my face from above. The light is so far away... I peer around myself and see cool, grey walls encircling me. Is it rock? I reach out to feel it. Cold, damp, and hard as stone.

What the fuck just happened? Where the fuck am I?

I pull my back up off the ground and feel every bone creak and moan in protest. I wince but keep pulling myself up, pleased to see that I can still stand. I was beginning to worry that the pain in my hips was going to keep me on the ground. Now that I'm up, I feel a whole new rush of pain. I fold myself in half and brace my hands on my knees. Jesus, I hurt everywhere.

When I can bring myself to stand fully I look all around me and try to make sense of what just happened. I take a deep sobering swallow as I realize the round stone tunnel that I am standing at the bottom of appears to be an old well now nearly dry from years of crap being thrown down to fill it. I glance down, kicking at the old rotting bucket at my feet, and know that I'm right. I am standing on a pile of junk at the bottom of what appears to be a 20 to 30 foot deep, old stone well. Fuck.

Fuck.Fuck. Fuck. I let out a harsh breath, a half yell, honestly. Now what?

This is just fucking great... How the hell am I supposed to get out of this bullshit? Somebody is going to have to come get me out. They have people that do that, right? They have to patrol the woods and help people that get lost and shit. Conservation agents or something. Isn't that a part of their job? If not, I don't know what the hell they're getting paid for.

I start shouting as loud as I can. Screaming. Yelling. Banging the walls. I am just making as much noise as possible. I throw rocks up toward the top, but they don't make it all the way. They come crashing back down on me instead. It's not going to stop me, but I think I'll throw smaller ones now.

I keep up the ridiculous ruckus for what feels like days. I know it has been at least an hour as I saw the sun move places in the sky. My throat hurts from screaming at the top of my lungs. I'm soaked with sweat and the scattered rain showers that keep pelting me with icy cold drops. I'm exhausted and frustrated. I lean back against the cold stone wall and give myself a short break.

Fuck, this is bad.

Who am I kidding? There is no one out here. There is no one coming for me. There is no one to help me but myself and that puts me pretty much up shit creek with no fucking paddle.

Realizing this makes me feel rage burning up my

spine until it explodes out of me in a loud growl. I throw another large rock up and have to jump out of the way when it hits the wall with a crash and rains down on me in smaller, now broken pieces. Fuck this.

I need to evaluate all my choices right now. What options do I have in front of me? Did my pack fall down here with me? A frantic search of the ground at my feet brings back the memory of seeing my bag flying away from me as I fell.

No bag.

Cell phones dead.

Not a single soul knows where I am.

Fuck.

Only I would land myself in a place like this. It's like a real-world representation of my current living situation. I let out a dry laugh. The literal and proverbial rock bottom. Maybe Karma is real and this is it.

I appraise my surroundings. It looks like I dropped about 25 feet or so. I feel my bones wince at the thought. I still hurt and I feel like my ribs might be broken, but I can still move around enough to function for now. Looking at the drop, I'm just glad to still be alive. I run my hands along the walls feeling the deep grooves between each stone. My fingers easily slide into the gaps and I'm sure my boots will have just enough room to balance on the very edge.

Without a second thought, I fling self onto the wall and begin climbing up the rocks. One after another I leverage myself up the damp and dark walls of my current prison. I should slow down and go easy, but I just want out of here. I claw my way up like a maniac.

I've made it up about halfway when I start to wear really thin. My fingers are beginning to ache and my body is reminding me how hard I hit the ground when I landed down here. My whole body feels like a giant bruise.

Everything hurts so much that it almost takes my breath away. With a shake of my head, I rally and reach up to the next rock. With a tight grip, I lift my boot to the next toe hold. My boots slip against the mossy wetness of the rocks and in my struggle to keep my hold, both of my feet fall away from the wall. Suddenly I am hanging onto the rocks 15 feet up with nothing but the aching tips of my fingers.

Inside I am nothing but panic, but somehow I manage to keep my body calm and still. If I let my body react like my brain then I am completely a goner. I don't even want to breathe and risk unnecessary movement. With excruciating caution, I pull my legs up to find a new ledge. With a hard kick I try to wedge my toe into the new opening. I smile as I feel my legs take some of the pressure off of my cramping hands. I let out a relieved sigh and begin looking for my next step. I've got this.

Just as I reach for the next rock with my left hand, I hear a loud crack and then a short pop. I barely even have time to register the sound in my own ears before I feel the rocks in my right hand give way and crumble to nothing. Again I am falling and there is nothing I can do to stop myself.

Time slows down and I see the glowing light of freedom slowly shrinking back down to a tiny spot out of reach. Worse yet, I see chunks of heavy rock that have come loose falling over the top of me. I think this is it. This is where I end.

As my body makes another hard splat in the three or four inches of water now covering the ground I hear another loud crack and feel a blast of pain in the back of my head. The pain is excruciating and I just want to die.

Maybe that's what I'm doing, I think to myself as my whole world fades to black.

I'm so cold.

My head hurts.

I am so cold.

Why am I so cold?

I'm shivering so violently that I think there may be an earthquake shaking my warm bed in my safe home until I fully open my eyes and see my own shaking form under about 7 or 8 inches of water now. Lying on the ground with my back propped against the wall, the water has risen to my waist and it is as cold as ice. The parts of my body that are under the water are now so cold that I can't feel them at all. I wonder for a minute if this is what hypothermia feels like.

I don't know how long I was out cold, but I do know that the sun has faded away and the hole over my head is nearly black with darkness. The only light is the soft glow of the full moon shining through the rain clouds outside of this hell hole.

My head is pounding. The pain is everything I can think about. I reach up with my numb and waterlogged fingers to touch the place on the back of my head that aches and burns like it is on fire. I can't feel anything my hands are touching, they are too cold, but I can tell that the back of my head seems to be... soft. Softer than anyone's skull should ever be. When I bring my hand back in front of my face I see it is covered in blood. That cannot be good. On the other hand, I still seem to be processing rational thoughts so that is a good sign.

A quick look over my surroundings shows that the rocks that fell with me have landed all around me, peeking out above the water level. Please, dear god just let me get out of this hole. The water has gotten even higher now and the rain is still falling. I'm so cold and so tired and just so done.

God, please. If you let me out of this mess I will tell Charlotte how sorry I am and how much I never deserved her. I'll call my brother and tell him I love him and he's the best little brother I could ever want. I'll tell him I'm so sorry for all the times I let him down. I'll tell him I'm sorry I left him with dad when I turned 18. I should have taken him with me. I just want him to know that I'm proud of him and who he is.

Jesus, if you let me out of this hole I will call momma and tell her it was never her fault that he hit us. It was never her I was running from and I'm sorry, more sorry than I've ever been for anything, that I didn't stand up for her when she was too broken to stand up for herself.

I'm just so fucking sorry for all the shitty things I've done to all the people I love. God, please just let me out of here and I will do everything I can to make up for all of it. I'll be better. I swear I'll be better.

Bending my head in shame and prayer I take notice of the fallen rocks again. Looking at where exactly they landed I suddenly feel a rush of panic in my gut. Where are my legs? I can't feel any pain from them being crushed, but now that I think about it I can't feel anything at all. Where are they? My mind tells my waist to bend so I can lean down to check my cold, wet legs but nothing moves. My breathing becomes shallow and quick as I come to the realization that I can't feel the lower half of my body at all and I don't think it is because of the cold. I pound on my thighs with my freezing fists and feel nothing.

My breaths come even faster now and still, I just can't fill my lungs up. I feel like the whole world is spinning. I feel like the bottom is going to fall out from under me.

Jesus Christ. I can't feel my legs.

Anger, anguish, and unconsciousness all descend on me at one time.

I slowly blink my eyelids against the daylight shining on my face. I wake up fully to see that the sun has risen and the hole over my head glows with what looks like delightfully warm sunshine. Down here in my little world though, it is still dark, damp, and freezing. The water level is now at least a foot and a half deep. It is up to my lower chest now, but at least the rain has stopped.

I glance down at my submerged legs and remember what caused me to freak out and hyperventilate myself to sleep.

A pained scream escapes me without anything I can do about. It is the sound of absolute torture. I thought I had hit rock bottoms before, but this is far beyond anything I could have imagined for myself.

In the few visits I have made to this sparse piece of public land, I have never seen another single soul here. The idea that I could yell and scream until someone hears me is beyond worthless. It may be months or even years before anyone walks past this particular spot in the tens of thousands of acres in the Mark Twain National Forest.

I think back to all the times Charlotte begged me to hunt closer to home because she missed me when I was gone and laugh. If only I had listened.

If I had listened to her pleas about all of my stubborn and asshole tendencies I might be at home on the couch with her on this wet and cold spring day. The two of us could have been wrapped up in a blanket together, completely tangled up in each other. Instead, I had brought her best friend into our bed just to prove I couldn't be tamed. I had laid her down on Charlotte's pillow more times than I can count, making her moan every time. I didn't love her. She was just something to do when I was feeling claustrophobic. I wish I had done all those things with the beautiful girl I shared my life with instead. I wish I had realized what I had in her while I had her.

Instead, I let her catch me with my face buried in another girl's pussy. She had screamed and cried. I had blown her off like it was no big deal because I'm a man that can do whatever he wants, fiance be damned. I had thought that she was trying to tie me down. She really just wanted to love me and I was afraid to let her. Break her before she breaks me I guess.

How fucking wrong was I?

I think for the briefest of moments that I have tears running down my face, god knows she deserves my tears shed for her, but instead it is rain falling on me once again. I turn my face up towards the gray sky and let the water pelt my face and fill my eyes with water. The world blurs and I wish it could carry me away. I wish I could forget who I am and how I ever ended up being who I am. I wish I hadn't let life turn me into this empty, heartless thing. I wish I had let myself feel all the things she tried to give me.

Funny how knowing you are going to die can put everything you have ever fought against into crystal clear perspective.

I think about all the times my dad told me to "man up" and deal with a dry laugh.

"Man up asshole," I say aloud to myself.

As I sit here in this hole, time seems to lose all meaning. It feels like it has been days since I landed here, but in reality, it can't be more than 24 hours at the very most. As quickly as the water has been rising since this batch of rain started, I know I couldn't have been passed out for more than a few hours after my second fall. If it had been any longer, I am sure, without any doubt, that I would already be long drown. Crazy how well this old dried out pit seems to hold water. Either that or it's seeping in from the ground under me. Whichever it is doesn't really matter though. These rocks on my legs have me pinned to the mountainous pile of discarded junk either way.

I'm so hungry. Ironically, thirsty too. Here I am sitting neck deep in freezing cold water and all I want is a giant glass of ice water. I would laugh at the absurdity, but I just don't have it in me.

I can no longer feel any part of my body because of the cold water covering me almost entirely, but I will take this feeling of numbness over the pain I was feeling. The pain from the fall was intense from the waist up, but as the water got higher overnight last night, that cold was entirely different. It was crushing. It was debilitating. It was so bad that, for the most part, I've been pretty out of it. I couldn't even stay conscious for it. I'm thankful for that at least and thankful for the numbness. I am now also thankful for the rising water. I know it will be what puts me out of my misery…

So tired…
So cold…
So hungry…
Just want it to end…
So, so cold…
Thirsty…
Cold…
Can't breathe…

Can't breathe...
Can't breathe!

My eyes fly open and water burns inside my throat and chest. I throw my head back as far as I can to pull my mouth above the water level. It's still raining, raining so hard, and the drops fill my eyes and nose. It won't be long before I can do nothing to keep my head above water. I knew this moment was coming, but I don't think I ever fully understood how it would feel. The internal need to breathe, to survive, is stronger than anything I can control. It's burned so deeply into our subconscious and we are helpless to avoid it as long as we are conscious. I want this to end. I want it to be over, but my brain won't let me drown as long as I have the ability to save myself.

The water is filling my ears now and making the world sound hollow and far away. Is this what dying sounds like?

I can hear what sounds like a man screaming in pain somewhere far away. It takes a minute of hearing the horrible wail in my ears before I realize it's me. I'm screaming and I don't even know it. I just don't have any other choice but to let all the horrible, awful things I'm feeling burst out of me in any way possible.

The water is on my cheeks and chin now. I can literally feel it rising higher and higher on my face as each moment passes. I tilt my head back even farther, enjoying the cold water on my crushed skull, but losing sight of what's above me as water begins to flood my eyes. My tears mix with the water and I think I can taste their metallic saltiness when the water slowly starts filling my mouth again. I close my lips tightly and breathe through my nose until the water slowly creeps up, filling my nostrils as well. I try to reach up with my arms and pull myself higher to catch another dry breath but there is nothing I can do but drown. I can still hear myself making some kind of wet moan and my flailing arms make the water splash and churn.

Suddenly I see a bright beam of light shining down on me and almost hear another voice calling out. My throat burns and my lungs feel like they might explode, but I stop moving and open my eyes through the water. I can see the wavy silhouette of someone in the circle of light above me. The water between us makes them look like a mirage. Somehow, though, I know they are real and they have found me.

They are too late.

All I can think, eclipsing even the pain of breathing in the strangling water, is they are too late. I watch them as long as I can. My almost saviors.

The pressure in my head is building, building, building. I can hear the person at the top calling down to me, but all I can think about now is how it feels like my eyeballs might explode.

All at once that pressure and pain inside me seem to burst open in an explosion of white light and scalding heat. Slowly the white light recedes into black nothingness and I hear laughter.

My dad's laughter.

Man, up asshole.

He continues to laugh in my ears and carries me into oblivion. This must really be hell.

Savior

"The real monsters have always worn a human face."
John Mark Green

Tall pines reach toward the amber sky as it fades to purple on a darkening horizon. There is a damp coldness settling over the hidden campsite beneath rattling tree branches swaying against an encroaching early November wind. Rebecca pulls the blanket tighter around her as the chill seems to steal away the campfire's heat. She already feels cold and dead on the inside. Keeping her physical body warm is essential to survival.

She feels the hot trail of a tear running down her cheek as the rustling tent behind her alerts her to her captor's awakening. They have been legally married for 17 years, but he would never be anything more to her than the invisible bondage tying her to a life she never wanted and hadn't been ready for. Since the implosion of their life just three days ago, Dale had ensnared her in actual real-life shackles as well. She was free to roam their campsite, but straying beyond a 6-foot radius in any direction would pull the chains around her ankles tight until they tear at her skin. She looks at the blooming purple and red rings beneath her restraints and hears the words he's been drilling into her since their wedding night.

Doing God's work is painful.

It was a lesson he instilled in all his wives and children daily. Sometimes the words were simply spoken in a moment of strife. Other moments, they were used to ensure obedience. He was one of the few chosen by God to lead their church and repopulate the planet with his seed, or so they had all been told. Rebecca had long ago stopped believing in the very existence of God. Dale's hand on her shoulder as he comes to sit by the fire with her is all the confirmation she needs. There is no God, but Dale is the devil.

"We'll need to continue our practice tonight," he tells her in such a reverent way that she is certain he must truly believe he is doing God's bidding. In reality, it is just his way to excuse away and justify the sodomy he will commit against her on this day. He calls it "practice" because the act cannot place another child in her womb, but still allows him to force himself into her as he has been doing for almost 2 decades. Over the years, they have "practiced" more times than Rebecca can count, but it continues to be a punishment that never gets any easier. Each time seems to be worse than the last, but there is never any way to stop it.

She simply nods her head in acceptance of his veiled command. The times she has tried to resist have excited him even more. He takes the opportunity to prolong her agony. It seems to give him joy to hear her cries so she works very hard to hold it all inside her, a discipline it has taken many years to perfect.

"The moon will be full tonight," he continues, "We'll travel as long as it gives us light. I want to be settled in our next campsite before sunrise."

She nods in agreement again, "Yes, Father Dale."

The use of his most preferred title leaves a bitterness in her mouth and he smiles at her discomfort. He gives her a long intentional stare from the crown of braids atop her head, down to her shackled feet.

"You were too slow on our trek yesterday and I wasn't pleased with how far we traveled. You must remember that doing God's work is painful, but we still must carry on through the pain. I will spare you today's practice until we have reached our new campsite, but I will expect penance for sparing you before we depart."

The words sting like a whip cracking against her bare skin. Penance often meant different things, none of them ever good. Bile rises in her throat as she chokes out a quiet agreement, "Yes, Father Dale."

His eyebrows arch over his aging eyes at her reluctant response, "And," he requests.

For the first time tonight, Rebecca lifts her head and stares into his eyes across the darkening night. Through gritted teeth, she forces out, "My pleasure, sir. Thank you."

He smiles at her dread and she is now certain she cannot go on living this life.

Clasping her hand in his own, Dale speaks, "Let us pray over our journey..."

Rebecca bows her head and closes her eyes, but cannot hear his words spoken to the God that forgot her a long time ago. Instead, she sends her own plea out into the expanse of the universe. Screaming in her own head, she begs whatever cosmic forces might be out there to save her and draw her out of this reality in any way possible. She has been sending this prayer out in hopes of response since the night she was married away to Dale when she was merely 13 years old. Now she knows this will be the last time she asks for salvation. If there is no hope for something bigger than this life she has, then her will to keep living will completely evaporate into nothing.

Tonight will be the night she stops going on in this imprisonment to patriarchy, one way or another. If no savior emerges for her before the sun rises over the treetops, she will plunge herself off the cliff's edge and into the river valley below. She can only hope the strength of her dwindling weight will be enough to drag her husband down with her as her chains tear him away from solid ground. She wants to end them both and let the fall carry them away into their own eternal darkness, but this night was going to have one last chance to prove the existence of something holy. Somewhere inside her is the last little spark of hope that has yet to be extinguished. She wants to believe, but her resolve to wait for Dale's demise is almost gone.

She is simply exhausted and has little left to give. She has lived her whole life in their communal church village, waking with the sun and working until darkness falls. Since they fled the chaos of their collapsing religious compound, they have traveled by night and only slept restlessly in hidden spots usually cold, damp, and home to another living creature that did not want them there. Even now, as they are just beginning their night's walk, Rebecca could curl up into a ball right here on the ground and sleep for days.

As the temptation to do just that peaks and she thinks it might almost be worth it, there is a rustling in the trees and brush all around them. It could be another breeze blowing through the branches, but something about it makes her whole body shiver. Her back has gone stiff and she slowly glances toward the edges of their shelter of trees with wide eyes. The rustling seems to be circling in on them as the leaves crackle all around. The air seems damp now and full of musk that clings to Rebecca's skin with a distinct heaviness. It is the smell of something wild.

"Wife! I expect you to work," Dale bellows as he sees her standing still as stone. With the sound of his command, the evidence of their observer seems to fade away into the distance.

"I think..." Rebecca stammers, "...sir, um... I think there is something in the trees."

Dale rolls his eyes and waves her off. His expression of frustration tells her to continue her gathering of their possessions, but she cannot shake the feeling that they are still being watched through a patchwork of bare branches and the last few crispy leaves of fall. As Dale straps her heavy bag to her back and the end of her chains to his waist, she peers around them hoping to catch a glimpse of the stalker. Finally, as they are making their way deeper into the wilds around them, she sees a quick flash of light alongside them. It was just a sparkle of reflected moonlight that she never would have seen had she not been looking at the exact right place at the precise right moment. The blinking orb of reflection is followed by a massive wall of gray peeking through the breaks in the brush alongside them. The grey shimmers and reflects the moonlight as well, but in a softer, gentler way. It looks as soft as clouds and she yearns to reach out and feel it against her callused skin.

Rebecca doesn't even realize she has stopped walking to gawk at the giant mass slipping almost silently alongside them until the chain at her ankles is pulled tight by Dale's momentum tugging at it. The tug is so forceful that her feet fly out from beneath her in an instant and she is suddenly slammed to the cold, damp ground of the forest floor. She lets out a yelp of pain as Dale bursts out frustration and pulls her body to him with a swift pull at the chain. She cries out as the dirt and rocks scrape across her skin and tear her clothes. Dale grunts at the effort with fury boiling out of him as he slams a hand across her face. She is sobbing now and clutches her already swelling cheek and eye. He stares down at her with rage and a still silence descends over the forest. The moment is heavy with possibilities and, for a moment, Rebecca is certain her spouse will kill her right here. Just as she becomes sure the end is coming, they both jerk their heads to the side and frantically search the treeline for the source of the guttural growl that just nearly shook the ground beneath them. Dale reaches for her hand and pulls her to her feet.

"Let's keep moving," he whispers by her side. He knows as well as she does that they have no way to defend themselves if something were to attack them. That is the whole reason they were traveling by night to begin with.

They are just two souls on the run with no way to fend off the authorities that Dale is certain are pursuing them. He believes traveling by night will make eluding them easier. The day they had fled had been the end of everything they had ever been a part of and they had no time to grab things to take other than a few essentials Rebecca now believes he had put aside in advance.

The end of their fundamentalist group had been coming for a while. Some girls had escaped and let the outside world know what it looked like to be a member. The FBI had been moving in closer for the last couple of months. The word "cult" was being thrown around and there were beginning to be whispers in the community. Fear was spreading through nearly everyone around them except Rebecca.

She was seeing a light at the end of the tunnel. If the government ended their commune, she and her children could be free, but then the bottom fell out from under her on that last day.

It was revealed that they would all be moving onto the next realm together. They would all take their own lives hand in hand and greet each other in heaven. Rebecca had been horrified. She could never imagine taking the lives of her own children. She began getting them out one by one that day. Sending them away, past the fences around them. She told them to run and keep running until someone from the outside found them. She told them that was the answer to salvation, get away.

She planned to join them as soon as she could get as many of the others out as possible, but Dale had found her first. He had been planning to flee with one of his own daughters. Rebecca had managed to sneak the 9-year-old child out before the plague of child marriage had claimed her as well. Dale was furious and had taken her instead. As he dragged her out into the wild that evening, the other remaining members of the church were falling to the ground dead in a suicide pact that would never make sense to Rebecca in any way.

He was certain the FBI would now be pursuing the two of them tirelessly and so they travel at night. It seems to be the only way to soothe Dale's warped and desperate mind, but now it appears to be their biggest hindrance as well. He hasn't seemed to think about what the forest becomes after dark until this very moment. It has finally occurred to him that when darkness comes, he is not the only predator sheltering in the foliage.

They have been lucky so far, only encountering sounds and the distant howls of coyote packs. Tonight felt safer at first, as the full moon rose bright and shining in the sky, but their luck seems to have run out. They can still feel the eyes of something watching them intently as they began a faster pace through thicker and denser areas. Rebecca knows it won't matter in the long run because the beast tracking them through the trees right now is far bigger and more powerful than any mortal government official could ever be in the bright light of sunshine.

Is it a bear? Surely that is the only thing in these trees that could grow to that size, but what about the color? Were bears ever luminously grey? Were there even bears in these woods? Rebecca has no idea.

The questions swirl frantically through her mind as Dale walks her faster and faster through the cluttered underbrush of a rarely traveled area. The further in they walk the harder it is becoming to just simply find a way through. She can feel the branches and thorns further tearing into long skirts until they are not much more than rags. Now the brush reaches out and pulls at her skin like greedy fingertips trying to hold her in place. She manages to continue on, but their chain seems to catch on something, suddenly yanking them both to the ground this time.

"God damn it," Dale howls as he tries to pull her to him by the chain again, but it has become too tangled between them now and whatever is holding it is holding strong. Rebecca can hardly even feel his yanks on her sore ankles now.

She takes this brief moment to lay her tired body on the cluttered ground to just breathe while she can. Once Dale gets himself out of the tangled brush and finds her, he is going to be so angry and she needs to prepare herself for the attack. She lays her head back on the layers of tree branches and leaves while staring up at the glowing ball of luminescence shining through the trees above her. The full moon glows so bright against the jet black sky that she feels the tiniest glimmer of hope for just a moment. Something in the moon has always offered her comfort somehow. It just feels full of promise.

As she clings to that feeling of hope, she hears a twig snap just aside her head. Her neck snaps to the side with a wince of pain but she is in time to see that same flash of soft gray passing by her faster than any animal she can imagine. Her breath feels trapped in her chest and her pulse thrums in her ribcage like the beat of a hummingbird's wings. She is certain it is beating loud enough to be heard outside of her body but the gray blur doesn't seem to notice as it comes to a stop between Rebecca and her husband, rising to its full and shocking height.

Rebecca hears Dale's horrified scream at the other end of her tether as they both take in the sight before them. Standing fully erect on its massive hind legs is a beast of massive proportions staring down the two souls below him, as if weighing their worth with his eyes. The growl coming from its elongated snout rattles the ground in its depth and intensity. Long, bone-white teeth protrude through a snarl with long strings of saliva hanging down into its matted, steely fur. Yellow eyes with red bloodshot veins coursing through them, stare down intently at his intended victims. Rebecca welcomes this obvious end to her story. She has been ruined by uglier monsters than this and she feels no fear as the creature uses a long razor-sharp claw to lift the center of the chain off the ground between them. The two are now suspended in the air, dangling upside down from the chain meant to imprison Rebecca, now going to be Dale's downfall as well.

Rebecca silently takes in this turn of events, but now looks deeper than just the sights around her and hears her husband's guttural sobs swaying on the other end of the chain. He is crying and begging for his life.

"Please… oh, god… please… spare me… please," he pleads through yelping sobs.

Rebecca's laughter spills out of her in glorious peals of glee. It's uncontrollable. Even with death undoubtedly upon her, the joy she feels through his pain is all-consuming. If she can watch Dale go first, she will gladly greet death with a smile. Her giggles only intensify as she feels the crushing blood rush flowing to her head as they both sway in midair like a pendulum.

The creature stares from the crying man to the hysterical woman and back again. As it seems to recognize the power shift before it, a sinister smile spreads across its canine face showing rows of overlapping and yellowed teeth. They could shred a full-grown man in seconds.

Leaning closer to Rebecca, the wolf's breath is sticky hot on her skin and smells of rotten earth. Seeming satisfied with his appraisal of her, the creature lowers the chain just enough to place Rebecca's back gently on the ground before snapping the chain in half. There is a metallic pop as the animal snaps it like a loose thread. Rebecca crumples into a pile on the ground and peers up at Dale being dangled before the wolf's drooling face.

Dale's former sobs have now become shrieks of terror and Rebecca explodes with profound joy at the spectacle. She has now come to think of this creature as her savior rather than a monster.

This hero brings her husband close enough to run it's long, wet tongue down the length of Dale's body, leaving behind thick strings of elastic saliva. It now reaches out with long clawed fingers and squeezes Dale's body like a vice. There are a series of snaps and pops that sound like heavy boots stomping through the woods, but Dale is now silent. His face is twisted with pain, but he can't seem to find the breath for screaming out his hurt.

Loosening its grip, Dale's face goes slack and his complexion is ghostly white. Tears stream down his face and he can no longer hold up his head. Rebecca's saving grace bares its teeth again in a lopsided smile. It is enjoying this immensely.

Realistically, Rebecca knows she should be afraid. She should be working to untangle herself from these chains and running from the scene, but she can't force herself to tear her eyes away from her husband's demise. She has already been dead inside since the first time her disgusting pig of a spouse forced her to take him inside her. He was a well seasoned 36-year-old man at the time. She had been only a child. He had killed whoever she might become in their marriage bed that first night and there was no future for her at all that was worth more than watching Dale's life slowly and torturously stripped away from him. She rose up on her weak and battered feet to watch rapturously as Dale slumped in the hand of her enormous hero. Broken from head to toe, he is only able to pitifully moan now.

The beautifully fierce wolf shakes Dale now. Like a rag doll, the man's limbs flail wildly as if he has no bones holding him together. One by one, this new canine friend takes hold of Dale's limbs and pulls them away from his body. As each limb tears loose with a wet crunch, the wolf holds the broken man in front of it while making a quick snack of each appendage.

Dale is bleeding out from every orifice of his body now, but the wolf is not done. It slams the limbless and bloodied torso against the ground again and again until even the pained twitch of breathing has vanished from the fragment of body left. The grey hero now pounces on Dale's corpse, tearing and slashing at the mangled flesh until there is nothing left.

Rebecca watches intently, refusing to look away until

every last shred of her abuser is gone from this earth. As the wolf finishes its meal, it slowly returns to standing over the now blood-soaked clearing. It turns its body to face Rebecca. She should be repulsed, horrified. It is covered in a thin sheen of sweat and blood all matting together in its fur. It is breathing so heavily that she is sure she can feel the warmth of its breath from 20 feet away. It stares her down, but she feels no need to flee. She stands her ground and feels secure in her place opposite the wolf. It seems different now. Its posture has become more human than beast and it begins to walk slowly towards her. In just three long strides it stands over her. Rebecca looks up at this warrior and feels so small she might disappear.

The hero kneels in front of her and looks into her face, still swollen from the hand of her abuser. Its breath is hot on her face and leaves a humid film across her skin. From this close it looks more docile than wild and she can't resist the urge to reach out and stroke the soft fur of its face. Her hero leans into this caress and softly groans in approval of the gesture. They lock eyes and share a look of complete understanding. They see one another's brokenness. They share a kind of heartbreak that few understand.

The wolf uses a gentle claw to pull away the remaining chain still wrapping around her ankles. She smiles at this kindness and embraces its neck like a child clinging to their innocence in a brutal world.

Tears roll down Rebecca's face as her new ally slowly turns away from her and calmly walks back into the dark treeline on all fours. Just before it disappears into the black night, it throws its head back and releases a melancholy howl at the round moon glowing in the sky above.

Rebecca gazes up at the white light in the sky as well and sees a whole new chapter of her existence opening up in front of her. A deep sob escapes her as she finds the first traces of peace within her since before she can remember. With a deep sigh and tears now freely flowing down her face, Rebecca slowly starts making her way through the underbrush and down the path toward a new life.

ABOUT THE AUTHOR

Amanda East is a lifelong lover of all things dark and scary. She has been watching horror movies with her dad and jumping out to scare her mom since the late 1980's.

She now carries on this tradition with her husband and their four children in the Missouri Ozarks.

Her first full length novel will release in 2020 and she hopes it makes your skin crawl.

Made in the USA
Middletown, DE
31 December 2020